The

GREAT
DEPARTURE

The House of Erydia

DeForest K. Mapp

Magnolia Dr. Books

The Great Departure, The House of Eryidia is a work of fiction. Names, characters, places, and incidents are creations of the author's imagination or are used factiously. Any resemblance of actual events, locales, or events or persons, living or dead, is entirely coincidental.

2014 Magnolia Dr. Books

Published in the United States by Magnolia Dr. Books

ISBN-13: 978-0692024553
ISBN-10: 0692024557
Editor: Melanie Terrel
Cover Art: DeForest K. Mapp
Printed in the UNITED STATES of AMERICA

www.thegreatdeparture.com

CONTENTS

PREFACE

I have often been intrigued with how women choose to go and explore other options when things go south in their lives, particularly in relationships. How they gather themselves and how they choose to move on after she's determined, "I've done all I can do. I'm done... I'm done!"

I have learned throughout my short while on *this* earth that how you feel one day may not be how you feel forever. But the cause for your liberal pause maybe indeed cost you everything that you have built with your significant other, and sometimes more.

What is the formula for not drifting apart? Is integrating your life to the point of be inseparable the answer? Or would that degree of closeness only pose too much of an obstacle in keeping your space? What is love?

I often question the very existence of the kind of woman that I need. Does she even exist? I will be forthcoming and admit that my imagination has created a wonderful place where *she* does exist. It's the place where I retreat to in between the women that I meet who do not pan out for whatever reason. Yes, I am working through my commitment issues. Thank God for the woman who understands that about me.

Every good woman should have the benefit of a man who loves her to the point where his thoughts about her are sweet, silly, and sometimes embarrassingly trashy.

But what happens when this type of jewel is found and then lost? Do you stay behind and wait for love to return? How long does one wait? When is it okay to simply just cut your losses and just move on? What are the rules in case you want to come back?

Acknowledgements

I know that parents are supposed to love their kids by default, but I could not have finished this work without the support and validation of my mother and father. Their unconditional love and believing in me gave me the added strength to endure many long days and late nights. THANK YOU, Mom n' Dad.

I also wish to acknowledge the acts of kindness of Bishop Kenneth C. Ulmer, Douglas Brown, Sr., Ronald Tatum, Jeffery Johnson, Jacqueline Boyd, LaRonda Morris, Demetrius Jones, Carolyn Washington, Gary Hardwick, Venita Roberts (RIP), Rhonda Chukes, Paula Roberts, Connie Mason, Garland Mobely, Techla Nesbitt, Hassan Napier, V. Nenaji Jackson, Greg White, Thelonius & Shenee Alexander, Ray Ivey, and Vernon Yancy, all of whom were instrumental in allowing me to remain committed. I sincerely thank each one of you. And I cannot neglect to mention the pleasant and accommodating staff of the Pasadena (*S. Lake*), Santa Monica (*Montana*), and Marina Del Rey (*Admiralty*) locations of Starbucks Coffees, all of whom were instrumental in allowing me to remain committed. I sincerely thank each one of you.

We didn't meet when we were supposed to.

The

GREAT DEPARTURE

The House of Erydia

Cн 1

A King stands upon his favorite fertile plateau where the ground is a unique mixture of clay and red soil that breathes fresh new energetic life. A cool breeze of wind pushes against his hairy bare muscular thigh from an easterly direction. He finds himself looking out upon a vast rich green fertile kingdom which lies far below. With all that has been given to him through divine order, this particular King stands with a decision that must be made. He thinks to himself, "How did it come to this? Creator beyond the here and now, please give me the wisdom, the power, and the strength to do that which must be done."

Four and a half billion years later, a woman awakens from a most strange anesthetic at Norfolk General. She comes to in what feels like was only a few short seconds that had passed. But it's been more like six hours. That was the required time quoted to Latrice Foster by her fertility specialist, Dr. Marla Vincent. "Latrice, how are you dear?"

Latrice had nothing to say, but it felt like she was just socked in the jaw but her entire body was feeling woozy and sluggish. Her head was throbbing and her body moved as if it were going through vegetable oil.

Latrice had made arrangements to have a car take her home after this fertility treatment, but just as she is being wheel chaired out onto the welcome carpet, her husband Rick pulls up in his white 66' Mercury Cougar. The abrupt screeching sounds of his stop does nothing but aggravate Latrice's monumental headache.

Annoyed, Rick gets out of the car and signals for the driver of the black Escalade to just move on. The driver just shakes his head and skirts off. None of this is how Latrice wanted this to go. Rick says to the nurse, "Hi, I can take it from here." The nurse backs up a little because Rick is clearly not even in the mood to be confronted, questioned, or for any parting instructions. He helps Latrice into the passenger seat of the car. He makes sure that her limp body is in and quickly closing the door, again not having any sympathy for her current fragile state.

He darts around the back of the car and just shakes his head. The nurse watches to make sure that his patient is okay. He doesn't have a choice.

Rick gets into the driver seat and pulls off, not having any real regard for how he's going over the speed bumps. Latrice is trying to keep from getting nauseous and mumbles, "Would you take it slow?"

Rick says nothing but he keeps on driving. Ten seconds go by and he takes it easy on the speed bump right before he leaves the parking lot. Latrice could sigh and relax. But then the dude pulls out onto Brambleton Ave. so quick that it almost causes him to get hit from the rear. He turns to Latrice and says, "What in the world were you doing there?"

Latrice looks out the window and sees blurry images, "Slow down!"

"What happened?"

"I do not feel like having this conversation right now." And the quiet tone that she responded in lets Rick know that she is indeed suffering from the pain of her recovery.

After they stop at the pharmacy to grab her prescription, Rick gets back in the car and he wants to say something. But how in the world do you argue with someone who is in pain?

They get back to their home and Rick makes sure that his wife gets inside of the house. Latrice tries to make it up stairs but she stops on the first landing and comes back downstairs.

She gets on the sofa and closes her eyes for a second. That second turns into four hours. When she opens her eyes, there's Rick sitting right there in front of her in the single chair, waiting.

"Hey, we need to talk."

Latrice mumbles, "Tomorrow."

"I thought that we discussed and agreed to you not undergoing any surgical procedures."

Latrice finds it easy to say nothing in response.

"Look."

"Rick, you act like you know everything."

"Stop. Just stop this is not about me being right."

Latrice struggles to sit up and she forces herself to sit and stare Rick in his eyes. "What? What! What Rick. What?"

"You made a promise."

"I had to make a choice."

"Whatever."

Such a dreadful night to have to face. Anything else that they've built together to this point has just disintegrated all together.

Rick leans up against the long floor to ceiling window, gazing out onto the headlights in their neighborhood. His breathing pattern and the moisture that's putting onto the glass is indicative of how unclear and misunderstood Latrice is making him feel. And since Latrice doesn't take his silence as a cue to try to go upstairs, Rick manages to say, "You just had to have your own way didn't you? It's incredible that... you just had to go on without me."

He's trying so hard to remain sensitive to Latrice's current state and she responds, "Rick, you didn't want to hear a damn thing she had to say."

"No I did not. We said that we were going to wait before we went ahead. Remember?"

Latrice tries to remember, but it's just no use.

What neither Rick nor Latrice was privy to was what went on during those six hours of Latrice being under. There were no doctors and no staff that performed any medical procedures on her.

After the anesthesiologist put Latrice under, the operating room and the team were completely prepared for the surgery. To Latrice's knowledge, it was going to be the removal of troublesome fibroids. But for whatever reason, Dr. Vincent was yet to arrive.

Then the unexpected echo of high heels increased as someone was advancing towards the operating room. The lights by which to operate began to dim. The peculiar look of uncertainty on the uncovered parts of the staff's faces broke the protocol in monitoring Latrice as well as the instruments that were connected to her.

Dr. Vincent comes through the double doors and holds them open as she stands. Refusing to come any further, her eyes begin to sparkle behind her designer frames, lightening to a hue of pulsating neon blue. Dr. Vincent then sends a pulse of high intense heat from her eyes throughout the room, targeting each one of the seven staff members, causing each one of their bodies to disappear, leaving a semi-circle of separate piles of blue scrubs and shoes. Dr. Vincent would never even enter the operating room all the way. She whips around in her white coat and leaves.

Dr. Vincent was the prey of a being from another time and space that was currently occupying her, and using her as a host. And that being's name was simply referred to as Five.

And he says to another being who actually taught him in his ways, "Rhaija, are you and your witchly cohorts ready to perform your ritual?"

"Well it's about time. I've been standing by forever."

"You are wasting time."

And in that instant, the operating room is filled with a sinister evil, one that has not been to earth since the fertile planet's inception. The seven seemingly beautiful witches that fall under the Spirit Rhaija's command all materialize inside the room, and they begin to immediately advance towards the helpless Latrice.

Hours after she's been revived and is back now at home, Latrice begins to feel nauseous. Her eyes begin to flutter rapidly, and she is hit with a sharp pain within the abdomen. And it takes every ounce of breath out of her body.

Rick slowly moves towards her. "What's wrong?"

Latrice rocks back and forth in Indian style, mashing in on her stomach.

Rick kneels down and says, "Try not doing that. If you press in too hard, it might rupture where they did the incision."

And then Rick lifts her favorite red cotton long sleeve shirt. To both their surprise, there's no scar.

Rick looks at Latrice. "What's going on?"

Rick is annoyed but he knows she's in pain. And as it builds rapidly, a tear comes forth from her watery eyes. And she falls over to the side.

And in that instant, Latrice's actual spirit is ripped away from her body, leaving the physical body limp, and Rick goes into a panic. "Latrice! Hey!"

But in the midst of that panic, Latrice's spirit is pulled helplessly from the house, into the air, and is requested far away from the earth's atmosphere. The innocence of her spirit was never meant or designed to travel across the vastness of the galaxy in this manner. That which mattered most to Latrice was Rick. And that which mattered most to Rick was caught somewhere beyond the Crab Nebula. Not even Rick in all of his knowledge on astrophysics has ever considered this as a possibility. He was on their sofa and she, at least the part that really mattered, was somewhere else, far away. Rick was feeling just as helpless while standing at the window, breathing out the warmth and moisture of his pain out on the window.

Meanwhile, Latrice's spiritual body was moving ever so quickly along a path that an earth being would liken to the DNA of the universe, or the Reesa. In a foreign measure of time, Latrice arrived at what her mind would consider to be a boundary of her home universe. The seven witches had performed a perfect spiritual anesthetic. But in this state of spiritual unconsciousness, she was permitted to be aware of what was happening. Her new eyes in which she now possessed sees a strange border, draped in a tall white curtain that extended itself as far to the right as it did to the left. She was amazed even more as to how far up it went. This border of the universe has so much puzzling simplicity, yet Latrice's mind was not able to grasp what it truly was. So much so, that Latrice could not even recognize the soft caressing hand of terror which was now extracting the very fetus that has been struggling to survive within her womb for five months.

Latrice did not move, for this calculated touch was a cross between Rick's tender embrace and the comforting way in which Dr. Vincent examined Latrice during those three visits. It felt so familiar that Latrice thought it was indeed just another medical office visit, the best of all visits, better than any prescriptive drug, and better than the deliberate touch of the tip of Rick's soft and strong middle finger. And all of that allowed Latrice's guard to come down and to surrender.

And now that she is near the Perimeter, the Spirit Rhaija has much more control. Her voice says to Latrice, "It's what you've wanted all along."

But none of these intergalactic mysterious beings had foreseen nor calculated the special bond that is shared between Latrice and her husband Rickland Foster.

Latrice opens her eyes to the harsh reverb of Rick's voice, "Latrice! Latrice! Stay with me."

In the next few minutes, her body is in the passenger seat of Rick's vintage sports car that has a few modern customized features. The clock on the dash reads 9:49:40pm. But those baby blue numbers blur in and out as a limp Latrice continues to remain loyal to this feeling of absolute submission.

Earlier that afternoon, an all-powerful, seemingly all-knowing spiritual witch had actually taken on the form the real Dr. Vincent. The effects of her dark sinister magic were now manifesting itself in real time as Rick sped Latrice to the emergency room at Sentara Hospital.

Rick was enduring and trying to manage his own trying moment, but he only had two hands. He had to drive down a busy I-64, try to get this Dr. Vincent on the phone, snap his fingers in Latrice's face to keep her awake, switch lanes around annoying drivers in the rain, cut his windshield wipers on, put the now ringing cell phone on his shoulder, and grab Latrice's weak hand. He was just as helpless as Latrice.

"Latrice!"

He ends the call, and because he's not paying attention to the road he slams on the brakes to keep from hitting the back of the car that apparently ran out of gas or something.

Meanwhile, in this part of unimaginable space, this strange powerful sorceress, Rhaija, is having her way with the essence of Latrice. It is only here that Rhaija is able to unleash her true evil power, according to her master. But there is another power who must weigh in on this matter.

Ch 2

On the other side of the Perimeter along another time line continuum, One who sees and understands everything must send one who just might be ready to see another who was distraught over her loss. Nothing like this has ever been done before, not in this universe or any other that has been created since. There was no contemplation necessary, for the almighty Creator understood more than others. But He knows that all outcomes must be at liberty to play out, even in His most remote place amongst every universe.

The time had certainly and finally arrived for an incredible meeting to take place. In the most undisclosed location of this universe, a discussion needed to happen in order for parties to exchange information. Invited, are two opposing sides and one Mediator who definitely stood for the cause of good. But He in His infinite wisdom understood like no other that some evil was still indeed necessary. "Good and evil would exist no matter what the circumstances were."

One was on the side of justice and two were for the side of evil. The time had come to have a special meeting between those who had a stake in the affairs of this universe. Typically, this would not happen because one side would not want to reveal their hand to the other, especially in the unresolved matter of the missing Yeswe'. But both sides trusted the Creator to keep His word that He would be fair, though He was surely for the side of good. Kaylandria, who had been saved recently by the Creator Himself, had to trust fighting along for her cause of good while taking on the task of remaining neutral.

The Spirit Rhaija asks, "Did Kaylandria truly learn her lesson for stepping into the Perimeter?"

As if this tormenting Spirit was truly interested in Kaylandria's care and protection. But the Creator knew the depths of Kaylandria's heart. Even though she never articulated her longing for more evidence regarding a personal epic loss, the Creator took on the weight of that anguish.

To think that the scores of millennia in which Kaylandria has served the Creator since release, no one else could have waited, and not complained, nor verbally expressed, while continuing to help others from other worlds, and have accepted that her unique but still privileged life was going to be just a little different from others.

And though this Creator knew that this was His perfect will, He was not without compassion or a sense of knowing how Kaylandria truly felt. He wept silently knowing how she chose to deal with her heart's earnest desire. For that pain of being disconnected from her original source had been suppressed so deeply that only He knew that it existed. The reward for trusting Him for over four billion years was about to be bestowed.

But before Kaylandria departed, she is first shown who she is, and to whom she belonged. And she is told by the Creator never to reveal that knowledge, for that was information that any Earth-being could not process.

Kaylandria was clear that she was now being allowed to return in her present state to the alternative universe where she had originated, at the time in which she departed from the Earth, something that she has been trying to do for an eternity.

Through the heavily monitored Perimeter, Kaylandria rejoices as she is set free by the Creator to go back into her own universe. She is being sent on her way to have just a few more moments than she did previously. This was the happiest moment in Kaylandria's most unusual life.

But elsewhere in the universe, today is the worst day imaginable for Rick and Latrice.

Cʜ 3

Taking time off for a doctor's appointment first thing in the morning never feels one hundred percent comfortable, no matter who you are. Latrice Foster works at a lobbying firm whose main special interest is putting an end to space exploration.

As she nervously meanders her way through traffic from Ward's Corner, she gets to the light and sees that she has an email on her phone, "Hi Latrice. Good morning. Could you come into my office please? Thanks."

That typical feeling of insecurity, "What the hell is about to go down?" befalls Latrice.

At 9:33, Latrice is pulling the cold sturdy glass door open to the office and walking at a semi-brisk pace. She starts to walk toward her own office, but Susan sees her from 40 feet away and stops her. "No. No. This way."

Latrice's inner thoughts run wild but she wrangles them in. "You got this girl. Just remember that."

Latrice walks confidently down the hallway and turns right into Susan Jaffe's office, Latrice's Vice President of Operations who she reports directly in to.

"Latrice close the door. And have a seat. I'm just sending my daughter a text 'I am… going to be home… early… right after… this… meeting.'".

But what Susan was really doing was sending her assistant a text, telling her, "Please peak your head in my office and end this meeting in fifteen minutes."

Making sure that her bangs stay out of her eyes and with a big apple lodged into her mouth, the assistant, Lucy, responds,"k."

Susan smiles and takes a quick breath, "So, Latrice how are you?"

Latrice is trying to sit on her nerves, but she knows exactly what's going on. "I just came from the doctor and I'm just dealing with a lot right now."

Susan's face lights up. "Oh, that's right. You checked on the baby! What's going on with that?"

Latrice responds, "We had a miscarriage."

Susan is so embarrassed. "Oh my goodness. It just happened?"

Latrice kind of quietly responds, "Yeah, that's why I took off and you've been kind of seeing me off and on pretty much for the last two weeks."

Susan adds, "Well, would you like to talk about it? I know the perfect fertility specialist, and she's right here off Granby."

Latrice interjects, "I think I'd like to keep this... yeah... I'd like to get back to work. I'm actually still way ahead of schedule for Tuesday's campaign launch, and I could probably help Tim with his solicitation."

Susan reaches over to the other side of her desk for a folder. "Well, your contribution is exactly what I wanted to speak with you on. I want to commend you on all that you've done. I think that me, you, Tim and everyone is in a good space on everything. The reason that I asked you to come in might be divine order."

Latrice is thinking, "I really cannot stand when you put your god into the mix of our conversations."

Susan continues, "Things have a way of aligning themselves at the right moment. Now that our project load is… has leveled out somewhat, we're doing some creative grouping in order to streamline our workflow efforts a little better. It's funny you should bring up Tim."

Latrice interjects, "I didn't mention Tim. Oh, right, Tim."

Susan cuts back over Latrice, "We're collapsing your position onto his."

This is the deadest pocket of silence that has ever attached itself to Latrice. And it's like the entire weight of the last two weeks are just hanging on the bottom of her jaw, as she searches for the right way to handle this.

But instead, she was quickly forced to reflect back on the news that Dr. Vincent just shared around two weeks ago, "I am so extremely sorry. But your body has rejected the pregnancy."

But Susan is in her office, with her elbows on the desk, legs crossed, one foot twirling because she's looking for the right words to say. "We've reached the end."

It's almost like Dr. Vincent and Susan were in on this together, and they bounced ideas off each other on how each should break the bad news to Latrice, all over drinks at a discreet dark lounge filled with cigar smoke as they sit on very manly tufted leather sofas. The 73 year old piano player would inspire all kinds of nifty thoughts on approaches for them both. And their night might have ended with Dr. Vincent and Susan stumbling across the street toward the parking garage attached to the Marriott.

Latrice is stunned and slips off into some other space in her mind. Dr. Vincent penetrates her thoughts and says in a nice calm pacifying voice, "Just get your belongings and get out."

But in reality, Susan is slowly waving her hand about a foot from Latrice's face, "Latrice, are you okay?"

Latrice's line of sight isn't the most direct. She takes a breath and tries to compose herself. "Well, I was under the impression that you and I were going to meet today at two to discuss, excuse me, present to you the ideas for a spokesperson."

Susan is intrigued. "Have you already started speaking with someone? I told you that we have a vetting process that we have to do before we speak to everyone."

"You know, I never understood your process."

"You could get into big trouble if protocol isn't followed."

"We're a new firm and you know that we make up rules as we go around here."

Latrice and Susan have a tendency to play tit for tat when it comes to name dropping. One knows just as many people in D.C. as the other.

Susan was connected to the Vice President of the United States, who just so happens to be rivals to Senator Ron Jacobs because of their stances on the new issue of ending the space program. This was a new issue all together. Who in the world was unhappy with the space program? Well on the Hill, whoever is in charge or desired to be in charge, had to come up with their own set of initiatives. And those initiatives should in some way be reflective of those in the highest elected office.

In this case, Senator Jacobs had aspirations of becoming Senate Majority Leader by the next election. And Senator Jacobs needed the Vice President's endorsement in key battle ground states, since he himself was favored to become the next President.

It's not that Senator Jacobs disliked the space program, just the opposite. His track record in the space program made him the most qualified to begin to dismantle it.

Why would he utilize his influence to do so? Simple, to attract and acquire more influence. In order for this to all work, this government funded space initiative would have come to a halt and retool it for the preservation of the environment.

All of this would now place Susan and Latrice at odds with one another. Susan was placed in charge by the Vice President, and Latrice was placed by Senator Jacobs as the number two in charge.

This shouldn't be any surprise to Latrice. But in light of the devastating loss of her pregnancy that she just experienced, another loss was just too much to handle. She was craving stability and peace.

Susan and Latrice stare at each other for a split second. Latrice sees her mother saying to her as a child while riding in the car on a cold morning, "Don't ever think about becoming a mother."

Susan isn't moved one way or the other. "Yeah, the point of the matter is, a decision has been made." Susan opens the folder and hands Latrice a pamphlet for collecting unemployment benefits.

She continues, "This was a hard decision to make, but look at it this way. Your benefits will provide your health coverage at your same deductible for the next 24 months. That's damn good."

Latrice tries doing quick math in her head.

Susan continues, "And trust me, I know how hard it is to start a family. And I know that's what you want. There are all kinds of options out there. Have you ever considered adopting?"

Latrice is thinking, "This nagging woman has one more time to patronize me."

The gravity of that sunken feeling of her loss was taking the wind out of Latrice second by second, but she was doing well in front of Susan, all things considering. "I've been operating within the bounds of my contract. And I've been very open and candid. When I had my surgery…"

Susan interjects, "Hasn't this been going on for the last four and a half years?"

Latrice wants to say something but now feels the certainty of Susan's abuse. "Check her!" "Who the hell do you think you are giving me advice about my body? This is my body, thank you."

And Latrice watches Susan just sit there with her thin bologna lips, nervously batting the vapors of her truth from her cheap mascara filled lashes. There is definitely some nervous energy that is building up in Susan's body. She understands that the rage of this provoked Black woman is ready to spill. But Latrice now keeps her cool, pulling all of her inner thoughts back.

Nervous and cautious, Susan decides to continue on the offense.

"These are sensitive women issues and I understand. But sometimes the best thing is to just allow the universe to take over and have its way. When things are happening like they are in your life, you just have to surrender..."

It's been exactly thirteen minutes and Lucy, Susan's assistant, pops her head into the office. "It's almost time for your 10 A.M. appointment."

Susan turns her head and smiles, "Thank you Lucy." She then picks up an envelope, stands up and walks toward the door, a nonverbal gesture that says, "Latrice get your ass out that seat and come on."

Susan then says, "So here is your last check. Don't go back to your desk. Your things were packed up and sent to your home this morning."

Latrice exchanges her swipe badge for her paycheck. It all felt so cruel and unfair. Knots in Latrice's stomach produced so much saliva in her mouth that she was swallowing it every ten seconds.

After Latrice leaves Susan's office, Susan then closes her door and plops down in her seat.

She takes a deep breath as she makes a phone call to a cell phone. It rings a couple of times. And she says, "It's done. She's gone."

A male voice says, "Good job. Latrice will be fine. But we had to loosen up some of the funds here for some possible extra campaign spending. Now when the election is over, I am going to recommend to the President, once he gets in office, for you to become the Energy Secretary."

Susan says, "Thank you Senator."

They hang up. Senator Ron Jacobs was just coming in from the golf course and now preparing to shower up. As he wraps his towel around himself, he thinks, "Latrice'll be fine."

He had a plan for her husband Rick, one that would ensure Latrice's security, as well as his own.

Cʜ 4

At that very moment, in another place that would appear very familiar, a stasis chamber has been kept at the necessary temperature for close to four and a half billion years, until now. His mouth and eyes may as well be glued shut. He's a motionless person of beautiful color and interesting outer features. His body temperature begins to go up. This function of the apparatus has not come on in a very long time. Originally programed and designed to accommodate the change in body growth, the incredibly well designed stasis chamber is now about six feet in length and about three feet wide. It's been purposely tilted at a forty five degree angle.

The conduits that run into his chamber run directly into the floor itself, into the simple but complex wiring of the basement, and eventually down into the ground. All of the nourishment that he's ever needed has come directly from sources natural to this place.

But he's eaten nothing. Instead, his appetite has been satisfied in part through his acute sense of smell. All of the necessary nutrients have gone to areas of the body where they needed to go. Asani had no say in this, but his eyes struggle as they begin to peel open. But it's so incredibly difficult. So much unrecorded time has passed since Asani has seen the light of day. And even then, he was only an infant. His memory is filled with images but with no real way of sorting through them, or for him to have the benefit to say, "Oh that's when this happened, and oh yeah, that's when that happened."

In the dimness of his isolation, he gets out of his chamber and falls out as he tried to use his butt to leverage his weight against the chamber. But between the dryness of his skin, the smoothness and angle of the chamber, Asani slides his way into a very clumsy and hurtful fall. It's hard enough for him to breathe as it is. And now he finds himself kissing the jaggedness of a dull walnut hard wood floor that needs some serious repair. Someone hasn't given any care to this room in a very long time.

Asani doesn't know what to look at, what to feel. He's so confused and disoriented. His feet are bleeding a little, he hasn't found his balance, and he's picking splinters out of his hand. Yet, he's up walking. But the trip to the room's corner is as far as it's able to go. And he stoops down in the corner to catch his breath. He thinks, "What's wrong with me?"

It is so absolutely unfair in terms of how he's feeling right now. He feels mad, confused, cold, and alone. And now that his other senses are active, his sense of smell can rest now. His sense of taste is now curious.

He shakes his head and just concentrates on what's in front of him. Asani stands nude at the door of the room. He now peeps his head into an even darker hallway. If it weren't for the light piercing through the window up ahead in a sitting room, Asani would not be able to see.

He is in a very traditional style single story ranch style home, something found in an obscure part of Arizona or Utah, like Monument Valley.

CH 5

Stepping out onto the front porch, Asani focusses his weak eyes onto a reddish orange sky. Who's to say what color it is? From left to right, there is absolutely nothing on the ground. A set of mountains prevail in the near distant, and that is where he puts his focus. He starts making his way down to the first step and then he falls face flat onto a pocket of soft sand mix. It doesn't hurt too badly. But Asani is definitely clumsy all over again. And to think, his parents took so much joy in teaching him how to walk. They used to joke and laugh about who would take the credit. Asani's memory had no problem reaching back to that tender moment. Blame it on the abruptness of that fall.

As Asani lays face down on the sand, a foot in what seems to be a quality black leather boot comes within inches to his face. One cheek up and one eye open, breathing as if his lungs had never been fully used, Asani looks up and sees a man standing over him, looking down upon him. This man with straggly nose hairs peeking out is Bowers, and he picks Asani up and carries his limp body back into the house. The metal adjustments on his suspenders that sit on his shoulders hurts Asani's chest.

He sets him down at the small table in the kitchen and whips up something that should help to reestablish his diminished senses and equilibrium. But it ain't much, a couple of crushed bananas and condensed milk, mixed together with a spoon in a sauce pot. Is the stove even on? This guy Bowers leans up against the stove with his pigeon toed self and stirs the next batch of his mix in such an irritated way that lets one know that this food is going to be horrible.

He drops the bowl down before Asani, and splatters a fair portion of it on him. But Asani's fingers are still very weak to be really meticulous about eating what's edible, and not on the floor. In fact, the portion that's on the floor, Bowers had already stepped through it.

However, Asani manages to spoon what's left of the liquid matter from the bowl to his mouth. Bowers walks out of the kitchen and leaves him alone. Asani wants some more. He looks around, almost wanting Bowers to do it again. "Give me!" He utters. "I..." But Bowers passes back through only to go back outside and he slams the rickety screen door behind him.

Asani has to get up and serve himself, a routine that is a little foreign to him. He goes over to the stove and starts eating directly from the pot. Bowers comes back in and snatches the pot out of his hand. "You do not eat from the pot!"

Asani tries to go for the pot and Bowers pushes it away. Asani comes back and tries reaching for the bowl again. But Bowers pushes him once more. "Get your pissy ass hands off me. Don't you ever touch me again! Do you hear me?"

Asani falls onto the kitchen floor. Bowers gives Asani another helping but sets his bowl down onto the floor, half of it is spilling out. As Asani lays on the floor still confused, Bowers heads outside once more.

Ch 6

Bowers takes four short trips everyday: one in the morning, two in the afternoon, and then one in the evening. After each trip, he comes home and prepares something for him and Asani to eat.

Actually it was just yesterday afternoon that Bowers was abruptly awakened from his sleep. His chamber is in the next room and he gets up with his precious splendor of life drawn from his body while instructions are still fresh on his mind from long ago, "Do not let this sun's shadow graze against any part of you."

And so now one day later, he's in Asani's face in the kitchen yelling, "I don't give a squat what you like or don't like. I say what and I say when we eat around here. And that's that. Would you care for something else? If so, take your monkey ass out there and go get it yourself!"

With a combat knife that has an interesting curvilinear design and insignia, Bowers easily cuts through some kind of meat he found and rations the skin and the liver out to Asani. He cuts into it with his twisted fork and the texture looks worse than a thick McDonald's hamburger, with the consistency of a moist cake. Asani decides to taste it anyway. He is so damn hungry. He puts this mess into his mouth and Asani quickly spits it out.

Asani's body is craving more and more nutrients and sustenance. He's trying to figure out, "Why is this person only giving me this little bit?"

It's almost been one full day and all of sudden Bowers feels an intense painful sensation. He throws his hands up and yells, "Why is everybody craving something all of sudden! Get off... just... leave me alone!"

Asani utters to Bowers, "Can I have some more?"

Bowers looks at him and says, "Hell no! You cannot have seconds!" And Bowers turns his back to Asani to cover up the bananas, milk, and meat on the stove.

Asani says again, "More!"

Bowers pretends as if he didn't even here him.

Then Asani jumps up and tries to reach over Bowers to get more food. Now, Asani is a bit stronger but he's still clumsy, but Bowers knows where everything is in the kitchen. He takes a wooden meat tenderizer with a big square block with rows of triangular ridges on each end and begins beating Asani's head. Again, Asani drops to the floor. And Bowers drops the tool and heads into another room of the house.

It wouldn't have made any difference had Bowers gone outside or just stayed put in the house. His particular stasis chamber settings were perhaps tampered with. Bowers and Asani were supposed to wake up at the exact same time, but Bowers was awakened early. Someone did this on purpose.

When Asani gets up from the floor, he gets curious all over again and decides to walk around the house. And he goes about the house in such a way that is absolutely annoying to Bowers. He's looking at Asani, but he can't see him. Bowers says, "I'm gonna say this one time. Do not touch anything that does not belong to you." And Asani takes his advice and walks around the house admiring it's very warm and bizarre décor as if it were a museum.

After each one of these trips, Bowers immediately comes back in and goes into a room where there is a 13" monitor and a strange computer key board, almost homemade. Think of an outdated Dell keyboard, and a monitor that resembles a *1984 Macintosh*. The lighting from the ceiling hits the workspace very delicately. The wallpaper is a soft hue of pinkish red with an interesting cream motif. There are hardly any wires.

Asani stands at the entry way of this semi dark yet beautiful room. He hears Bowers say, "I would appreciate it if you did not stand over my shoulder."

And Asani leaves Bowers sitting at his screen. He waits until Bowers is gone, and he comes back to the opening of the room and just stands, and stares.

Ch 7

"I don't know who you thought you woke up to, but if a nigga don't work, he don't eat. I ain't your momma. And I damn sure ain't your daddy. The only reason I'm here is to make sure your ass don't die. That's it! It's that simple." These are the typical words that Asani would begin hearing from Bowers. Who is this person and why is he trying to be this sort of wicked slave master?

Five, the sinister being responsible for Bower's mental abuse, has been misusing the power and knowledge that he has collected through his ability to travel from one time period to another. While the Perimeter was off limits to some, Five certainly learned its mystery while serving his master, Onjito. And though he now serves a new master in this present day, he is able to move about a little more freely, while having a new found slave of his own. While Five was scouting for remaining fragments of the Yeswe', an accident occurred and he made a huge miscalculation in his time-jump from the Perimeter and he discovers an era on this Earth where blacks were transported from a home continent of what was called Africa and sold to a place in the Americas. This miscalculation in his travel triggered a temporal distortion field which caused the stubby little Five to experience diminishing glimpses of a race. A race that he knew had once ruled the Earth. Five was amazed, astonished, pleased and empowered as he noticed how this people's displacement had triggered a downward spiral. And this spiral would lay the foundation for separation. And Five would use every nuance of information to his advantage to first see himself from his Master Onjito. Second, he would use this fragmented knowledge of slavery and the civil rights era as the advantage that he needed to prevent the heir of the Earth from returning to power.

Five has now found a way to wickedly streamline the purest in negative thoughts of all Blacks into Bowers' mind by casting one of his most powerful spells. By harnessing the power of the Perimeter and understanding his initial mistake in time travel, Five was able to create a porthole to the place where Bowers and Asani have been hidden since the 2nd Departure.

How does one travel to a destination without knowing the exact location? This was the mystery of the Perimeter.

Meanwhile, Asani scurries off in his own necessary moments of pleasure and curiosity, but Bowers catches him daydreaming and slaps him on the back of his neck. "Don't be turning your back to me boy." Bowers wants to control Asani at all costs. Bowers is a tyrant... a dictator. "It's my way, you idiot, or no way at all."

It's all about food, clothing, and shelter. Asani quickly understands this. He has to use a lot of energy to pump what really isn't the cleanest of water in order to quench his thirst. Asani's throat is anything but moist, causing his breath not to smell that great. After all, he is human. It's hot as hell out there. His neck is sweating, his veins are pulsating in his forearms, and his eyes are burning with irritation.

Bowers instinctively decides to stroll on over to Asani in this anguished state. He's so quiet and so on edge that it doesn't even seem to bother Bowers. But then Bowers looks at Asani with a moment of intense sympathy and regret, as if he himself had done something wrong. And these duplicitous feelings create some inner conflict. It's as if something is not right with Bowers.

All of sudden and on cue, a quick shock jolts up Bowers' spine, immobilizing him long enough to hear the bidding of Five, the being who is actually responsible for tampering with their chambers.

The spell that Five had put over Bowers allows thoughts to go from him to the other. The shocks to the brain are so effective that it makes Bowers obey Five's instructions. And Asani of course does not know the difference.

But Five's search is nowhere from being over. However, others do know that he has come closer than anyone in knowing where Bowers and Asani have been. A lot of patience has finally paid off.

"Ain't nobody tell you to keep your ass in that lil' special bed for all this long time. Feedin' you like you some patient in a hospital. So now, take your ass outside and figure out how to give your body what it needs. Go head... bye!"

Asani can really start with a good bath, but he's still hungry.

So he wanders outside and tries eating raw dark life filled dirt, a pinkish worm finds its way to the top before he puts the handful into his mouth. He immediately chokes and spits it out.

Bowers laughs, "Tastes good doesn't it? I bet you won't put that dirt in your mouth again. That's what the cables are for stupid... it filters all the trash out." And he was right. The vast network of cables that ran beneath the house and into the ground, filtered everything and turned it into recognizable food. There is about a 10 to 20 percent margin of error. But Bowers' really cannot cook anyway. So it really does not matter.

But Asani's senses... especially his sense of taste are beginning to yearn for more. Even while his body is in this perpetual state of discovery, it's very much confusing as well. It is like knowing what you want and not knowing where to get it. And then that conflicting duality of Bowers' personality acts up. And he says to Asani, "Boy you need to get your ass in that house. You don't need to be hangin' outside." Asani continues to stare out into the vast openness.

About 75 feet in front of him he sees something obscure on the ground. But he can't make it out. And then Bowers comes towards him. Then Bowers, who stands five inches taller, looks at Asani. "What I just say?" He then grabs his arm, "I said bring your ass inside the house right now. You hear me boy?"

Asani is so confused by Bowers. "Who is this... person? And why does he call me nothing other than my name? Who am I? What am I supposed to be responding to?

Poor Asani, even he sees the difference in Bowers' behavior.

And while sorting through this confusion, he's being told very specific things by Bowers, "Hey boy, look at me. You gotta trust me. I'm all you got. Ya hear me? If I do or say something to offend you, you're just gonna have to get over it. I am under a lot of stress."

This stress is the work of one who has been watching, looking, and trying to find an advantage to score the biggest win of the entire universe. In any isolated case of taking power, time has no relevance, bearing, or significance. At any given moment in time, there will be a winner, and that means that there also has to be someone else who loses.

C_H 8

Moments later, Latrice pulls up in the driveway of her two story brick colonial style townhouse and her blue front door is wide open. She gets out of her burgundy Porsche' with her cell phone already in hand. She calls 911 and begins frantically reporting a burglary. And then she walks in and discovers that the majority of the furniture is gone, no flat screen, no refrigerator, no treadmill. She's never seen her beige carpet so bare. But the white ceiling fan is spinning on a low setting. It felt good in the house.

A calm voice of a single fifty-two year old black woman on the phone says, "911 emergency response, how can I help you?"

And the light bulb quickly comes on in Latrice's mind. "Uh, no, I'm sorry. Let me call you back. I didn't mean to call you." Latrice hangs her cell up and places her bald up fist on her hip while she taps her finger on her chin. Oh but she is hot.

She's mad as her lips get right as she thinks, "That motherf' better not have done what I think he did." Latrice then dials another number. She goes and leans herself up against her favorite butterscotch painted wall that leads up upstairs. The phone is ringing. It's the call that she's really been dreading to have all day. Her stomach cannot take another dose of pain, but the butterflies seem to make their way around.

Latrice goes straight to voice mail. "You've reached the voicemail of Rickland Fost..." And Latrice rolls her eyes, breaths, and hangs up. And then she waits a second and then decides to call back, gets his voicemail again, begins to hang up, but she decides to leave a message. "Call me." And then she hangs up.

This dude, Rick, has literally cleaned her out, leaving Latrice the bed upstairs, towels upstairs in the hall linen closet, cleaning spray under the kitchen sink, the dishes in the sink (with food on them still and cooked by the sunlight), one love seat downstairs, and a bunch of fiction and self-help books which do belong to her. What else could happen?

There's a knock on the door. A white man with a Maytag looking outfit tries peeking through the top of the door. Latrice sees him from the stairwell and he yells, "Looking for Latrice Foster."

She opens the door on him with her forehead all tensed up. He says, "I have a delivery from JM National." And he literally just drops the box just inside the door. Latrice just shakes her head in disbelief at how big and unstable the soft cardboard box is. The packing tape was just so whatever.

She slowly begins unpacking the box. On the floor lays a framed black and white picture of a happy Latrice and Rick, awards, trophies, paper weights, and two pair of her favorite high heel shoes. Latrice then lifts the picture of her and her husband Rick, and just stares, wondering. "Is he okay? That punk ass. Does he need some money? I know he does. Let me check the account. He's always asking me for gas money. Who's he staying with?" So Latrice gets up and finds her cell phone, and she thinks, "I wish he would have called. I really wish I would have seen a missed call from him. But whatever."

CH 9

Shonnie, Latrice's longtime friend since Churchland Academy Elementary, comes in with food. She goes to the kitchen and notices that Latrice is just distraught. She notices that there are hardly any plates, but finds a couple. Within a few minutes of washing and then drying their hands on their butts, they're in the middle of the floor eating take-out from Momma Chan's.

Shonnie asks, "So you wanna talk about it?"

Latrice digs in and unleashes herself into each bite full of shrimp fried rice. "Not really."

Shonnie knows she's in denial. "Okay."

Latrice could be mistaken for the perfect picture of greedy concentration, but this time Shonnie gives her a pass. But Latrice's eating doesn't last for long. Sitting legs crossed in Indian style, she puts the plate down and just holds her head, "I can't believe that he's not even here or even checking up on me."

Shonnie comes over to hand her a paper towel. "What do you mean this time? Why did he leave?"

Latrice wipes her mouth and takes a deep breath. "I mean it wasn't even a real reason. A couple of days ago he left his Facebook account open and he was rushing to go to work. So I..."

Shonnie puts her face down, "You didn't."

Latrice can't look her in the face. "Yes I did. I went into his Facebook account."

Shonnie's nose starts to itch a little and she scratches it. Here comes a sneeze. Latrice throws a napkin at her. "Bless you. Yes I did, and I went into his inbox and saw all these women that he's been communicating with. And he's saying the same thing that he's telling me."

Shonnie, who isn't as limber as Latrice, just leans back against the love seat. She looks up and starts messing with her braids. They're not in the way but this is just how she piddles as she thinks.

"Okay I'm listening." Latrice is looking for the remote. "He took my flat screen. Anyway, he's friends with more women than..."

Shonnie is listening and interjects, "What kind of women?"

Latrice starts snapping, "What do you mean what kind of women?"

Shonnie holds her tongue, but asks, "Were they young, old, skinny, white, rich?"

Latrice responds, "What difference does it make? They weren't me."

Shonnie calmly responds, "People and these stupid Facebook accounts. I guess if he were the one pregnant, he wouldn't have time to be all up on Facebook." And Shonnie holds her head face still. Her eyes look straight into the heart and mind of Latrice, creating a heavy raindrop of truth from the now still ceiling fan, almost ready to drop. She had struck a nerve with that word, pregnant.

That clear dewy drop of rain does indeed decide to fall. And when it does, a thunderstorm makes way for an intrusive bolt of lightning outside. Where in the world did these overcast clouds come from?

The lights go out in the house, leaving Latrice and Shonnie in the dark. And while Shonnie is asking,

"Silly question, but do you have any candles?" Latrice is taking a mental trip back into the room with Dr. Vincent. Dr. Vincent just leaves the room. And the room goes completely dark, cold, and another door appears. It's probably just an insurmountable amount of bitterness that could overtake Latrice. She stoops down and gets under the cold metal uncovered unpadded examination table. Life should be so much more abundant and pleasant than this.

Shonnie has crawled around and was fortunate enough to find three votive candles in the cardboard box. "Girl where's your lighter? Forget that. I ain't crawlin' around here no more."

So Shonnie finds Latrice curled up into a nervous rocking ball teary eyed under the dining room table. Shonnie goes underneath the large table to keep her company. "Hey."

Latrice turns her head to Shonnie, "I lost my lil' her."

"Shhh." Shonnie gets right next to Latrice to comfort her dear friend who is closer than a sister. She takes her rather large hands with medium sized nails and nurtures Latrice by running her hands through her hair.   Every second, Latrice produces one deep irregular breath after another.

And her breaths get even heavier. "I so wanted this to happen for us. He would have loved me if I could have done this for him. I know how much he wanted this to happen. I needed this to work out. I knew that if this time wasn't going to work he was going to leave."

Shonnie asks, "Well when did you tell him?"

Latrice continues to clutch even more so onto Shonnie's rather large warm arm and then she lets go. "I didn't tell him. It's what I didn't say. I know Rick and he knows me. If it was good news, I would have called, but since I didn't, I think he knew."

Shonnie can't believe what she's hearing, "Yeah but... that doesn't make any sense. Who leaves when they don't hear any news? His ol' punk ass just wanted to leave."

Latrice gets up and then Shonnie gets up and they both go over to the front room window. She pokes her fingers through the blinds to observe the warm rain storm pouring outside. The occasional flicker of lightning provides a little more light into the house.

Latrice shakes her head while gazing and says, "Rick got so angry when I came to him and told him. Rick put the blame completely on me. And started talking all this stuff about how we would be in a better place if we were more open about having kids a while back. I guess I did it because he's so closed off now. I told him that I was sick of him marginalizing me to this one area of his life. And then he says, 'Regardless of what you have or don't have you have no right to go into something that does not belong to you."

And Shonnie looks on with her arms folded and eyes squinted. "Y'all are still on that Facebook mess. Can't blame him though."

Latrice gasps and twists her head over to Shonnie, "Well whose side are you on?"

Shonnie responds, "You know damn well if someone went into your stuff, your belongings, your purse, you'd be upset. Now let me say this, him moving ain't got nothin' to do with no stupid Facebook account. Let's be clear about that. He used that as an excuse to do something that he wanted to do." Latrice rakes her hand through the blinds, almost tearing them down. "Exactly." And she coughs from some of the dust that's accumulated.

Shonnie says, "Did he clean? Anyway. But my point is you did something you had no business doing. And Rick then took that and pretty much said 'Look at what I did... but look at what you did.'"

Latrice is halfway listening. It's so hard for her to concentrate right now. She's back to piddling with the trim around the window as she leans up against her beige wall that she and Rick painted last year.

Shonnie says, "Do you think he needed this baby to make your relationship work?"

From the hospital, to Dr. Vincent's small office with the green walls, to Susan's office with the blue walls and endless stacks of paper, Latrice is reliving all kinds of moments from the last 24 hours.

"Yes." She sees Rick on top of her in their squeaky bed the night she knew he impregnated her. She cannot get rid of the image of the way he would lock his fingers together and hold her head up like a pillow, making it easy for her to see that vein in his forehead while he hit her spot just right. "I knew when it happened. I looked at him and he looked at me while he was on top. And with his eyes, his eyes only, he asked me 'Will it be? Will it honestly be? Please say it'll be so.'" And Latrice's eyes, filled with the mystery of the universe, said gently to his pumping heart what it needed to feel. Then they calmed down.

Latrice continues to say, "But somewhere something got lost and he saw what he needed to hear. He gently got off of me and decided to stay. We curled up in a ball for two days straight it seemed. Everything was right. And I wanted to have his closeness forever. I did not want to get up. I so love him. He didn't need for me to tell him anything. Now that the baby is gone, everything was gone. And neither one of us had to say anything. Sounds weird, but, that's how close we were."

Shonnie is bothered. "Yeah but if that's all he was with you for, what good is that? Do you know how selfish this all sounds? You're a person."

Latrice's active mind falls upon the morning of her horrible discovery. She remembers standing in Rick's very well organized mahogany walk-in closet. Rick opens it and takes her out and stands her off to the side so that he can get a better glimpse of his suits and ties. It's not even a big closet. But she had something that she had to get off of her chest, and he wouldn't let her.

Shonnie continues, "Why didn't you tell him?"

Latrice responds in a whine, "Because I didn't know. I didn't know."

But she did know. Latrice felt closer with this peaceful child that she was carrying than anything ever before. And in a strange way, Latrice knew that the child felt the exact same way. The inside of Latrice, as far as the child was concerned, felt better than the highest quality thread count of any luxurious linen. The only person who could come close to even understanding this comparison was Rick. Oh how he loves placing himself inside of her warmth.

Cн 10

Rickland Foster is just a few blocks away at the Freemason Abbey eating dinner, looking out the window as a hard Tidewater rain comes batting down. And then his phone vibrates on the annoying crease of his white table cloth. He looks down at it and the screen reads "Latrice". He touches the phone and just shakes his head in his own disappointment. He's not so much mad at her as he is himself for being mad at her. His unchecked emotions are too much for him to handle. So Rick articulating how he actually feels is absolutely out of the question. The night that has approached takes Rick's line of sight out onto a rusty barge on the Elizabeth River. Rick's mind drifts in the same manner.

For the past two years, Rick has been working tirelessly in the privacy of his research lab that the U.S. Air Force Base has provided him at *Hampton University*. Senator Ron Jacobs thought it would be an excellent idea to utilize the seclusion of a small Black university to conceal Rick's work. "If you need anything else, I'll make sure you have what you need over at Langley."

And Rick thinks for a second and responds, "As long as I can teach a class."

Senator Jacobs responds, "A class in what?"

And per that agreement, several weeks later, corresponding to the academic calendar of Hampton University, Rickland Foster stands before a classroom of physics students, saying, "Where do we evolve from? Where do you originate? If you have problems figuring that out, ask yourself 'How did you get here?' Personally, I often wonder, 'What I am today?' Is it more or less than who I originally was?"

"Who is responsible for what we have today? The entire concept of buildings, beds, streets, food, water, newspapers, chairs, desks, lamps, cars, boats, did the ingenuity of our mind take us to its proper destination, or did it detour us away to where we are now? And where we are now, is it a mistake?

A student in the middle of the lecture hall asks, "But this is the world in which we made."

"Exactly. I often wonder did we miss the mark at some point. And if that is the case, is the world that we made the world that was intended? If the world was attached to another intention, whose intention was it to begin with?"

The same student asks, "I think people that think that like might be depressed or just hates life."

Rick considers that thought, "Interesting. So you think that if I or anyone forgot about any issues that they might have, that it would cause me to appreciate life?"

"Well, maybe, yeah."

"Now, I love life. But it doesn't mean that I do not give myself permission to ponder and wonder other possibilities, other concepts, and other universes. How is the one universe that we have been told existed, how is... was it orchestrated? Welcome to Exobiology 400, 'the study of life elsewhere in the universe'. Forget the prereqs. All that is required for this class is an open mind."

"What are the obstacles to an open mind? Anyone?"

A student responds, "Fear."

Another student responds, "Lack of information."

Rick responds, "Why should a lack of information prevent one from having an open mind?"

That student says, "Well if you don't have the right information to make the right decision, then it is irrational."

Rick responds, "Which source of information will you choose?"

Another student says, "Which ever source is the most accurate."

Rick says, "What do you mean accurate?"

"I mean it…"

"'It' what?"

Rick, when inspired by the passion of others, can provoke from any student who was as passionate. "'It' meaning the mission or the quest to get to where I think I should go or be."

Rick sits on his desk with his back hunched over a little, "Brilliant. A quest or a mission is fueled by your need, your passion, and your purpose. A little bit more than maybe what you signed up for, but this is why I am teaching the course and not someone else. See you next class."

Rick takes his coat and class attendance and leaves as the class follows.

These discussions are all very meaningful if for no one else but Rick, who has been working on solving a very complex set of algorithms that will hopefully allow a person to travel from one time continuum to another.

Everyone including Senator Jacobs thought it to be lunacy when he first introduced the theory. It was not until graduate school at the University of Maryland that Rick had his first breakthrough. He was able to make an object disappear for a time period of 2 seconds. But when the object reappeared, its original state had been altered. There was rust. Rick's professors came down a little hard on him because in their minds he was wasting scarce research money.

Sometimes he would come home to Latrice and she could tell that his mind was stuck somewhere else. "What's wrong with you?"

And when he would tell her what had happened, she would actually get very excited. So much so that she would go and tell Senator Jacobs the next day at work. "Rick's not sure that it can work, but I think he's onto something."

Ron would then say, "Well tell him to call me."

Latrice would then respond, "He's not going to do that."

"Well, why not?"

Latrice knew that she had no business opening her mouth. The last thing that she needed to hear from Rick was that she was meddling. It's not anyone's business what Rick was doing. Latrice loved the fact that Rick had aspirations to walk among NASA's elite, namely because it meant a degree of status and security that Latrice would love to have.

But Rick's work was not just steps along some trite career path. He was very much connected too its meaning, its purpose. His Inspiration might say that it was connected to his own faith.

Rick being in the lab and translating his problems and theories into mathematical equations, it was very spiritual for him. And so anyone not connected to where his heart truly was, just did not receive the full benefit of his knowledge and passion. The exception might be with his students, depending on how Professor Rick Foster felt.

He very much enjoyed the exchange between him and anyone who was serious about learning. It truly was a mutually beneficial experience.

One night Latrice walks in from work where Rick is just home chilling. Rick says, "So lay it on me. What's this news?" And when she tells him she's made arrangements for Ron to come by and see some of his work, Rick just looks at her.

With a warmed up bowl of Rick's delicious veggie soup, Latrice says, "What?"

She knew what she had done. Rick is now giving Latrice the silent treatment through this early part of the evening.

But Latrice knew that what she had done was the right thing to do. "I just want someone to help you. What's wrong with that?"

Rick just sits on the sofa trying to get into one of his favorite times of the evening, NBC Nightly News. The music leading into the news show was enough to get Rick's undivided attention. Brian Roberson was reporting, "Good Evening. Today was a day for a shocking discovery in what experts consider a breakthrough in the field of medicine. A link has been made between the concentrated intensity of the sun's heat in Africa to the reason why over 75% of the world cases for sickle cell anemia can be traced there. Kristen Bowen has more on this story. Kristen..."

The story then shifts to Nigeria where Kristen, is standing by in very light weight but colorful clothing. No matter how much the production truck and producer has tried to shield Kristen from the sun, her eyes continue to squint. But though her eyes are partially open, it does not prevent them from telling the story that she cannot get out of her mind. "Africans, people, children, infants, and adults, suffer from a disease that has been the talk of many decades, Sickle Cell Anemia."

Latrice comes in dressed with one of Rick's good dress shirts on. He says nothing. She grabs the remote and changes the channel. He still says nothing. But

Latrice pretty much knows what he's thinking and she says, "I don't want to watch anything depressing right now."

The opening credits for Star Trek Voyager come on, and it puts Rick in a slightly warmer mood. And then he surprises Latrice by snatching the remote and changing the television back. And Kristen says, "There's a fragment in this village that the natives found and have kept for the past three days. And the effects are remarkable."

Rick watches an amazing interaction between two doctors and a beautiful little girl, 12 years old. She was born with sickle cell but there are no traces of her ever having it.

Rick says, "Look at her. Everyone there should be that happy."

Latrice responds, "Happiness is a choice."

Latrice wants a kiss but Rick gives her like the corner of his mouth.

His eyes and ears are still on the television as Kristin continues, "A miracle in question, but the UN says that tests should be done. The strange rock has attracted the eyes of good and evil. In this part of Nigeria, there are those who have heard of the mysterious Miracle Rock and told us here at NBC that if you want to be healed, you better come ready to deal. Fortunately for this village and others across the continent, the United Nations moved in with its special forces unit and retrieved the rock which is already being called an ancient artifact. Senator Ron Jacobs from Florida, who also serves on the United Nations Environmental Council, had this to say from Washington, 'This is a brilliant discovery that we will get to study more closely here and hopefully determine what this is.'"

Rick says to Latrice, "There's your boy. All over it as usual."

"He's not my boy."

Meanwhile, in other far away parts of an unaligned realistic universe, Onjito sits upon his throne in deep meditation with his back to his crew on his starship. He thinks to himself, "No. It cannot be."

Onjito's chair revolves around slowly as he speaks to his 2nd in command, Five. "Tell me Five, why was I not ever told about a fragment of the Yeswe' still on Earth?"

"Why, that is impossible."

Onjito calmly says, "It is not impossible. You simply did a poor job. Four billion years ago and your lack of attention to detail still catches up with you."

The dark ruler rises and then descends down the steps from his thrown. "I want you to assist Dr. Foster in his endeavors."

Five responds, "You heard the Creator. No one is to touch or harm Rickland Foster.

Onjito says nothing.

"Yes master."

"Come here."

All of the hideous armored guards with their weapons slowly take a step back from Five. And Five fretfully moves forward. Onjito says, "Closer."

And all of the guards take yet another step back.

"Yes. I am aware of what He said to me. But He did not say anything about anyone else. You see, I know that you were listening in on my very private meeting that the Creator had called. Based on the Creator's rules of engagement, my instructions to you are to inhabit the conscious and spirit of this trifling one called Senator Jacobs. Rip his spirit out. Do what you enjoy doing the most. Become him so that you can get into the ear of this Rickland Foster."

Five understands his master's plan.

Onjito continues to say, "Since the Creator set forth His protective rules, I have been studying every facet of Rick and Latrice's lives, searching for a flaw, a loophole."

Onjito understood that if Rick was somehow eliminated, then Latrice would not be a factor. Onjito also sees that Latrice is the object of battling affection between Senator Ron Jacobs and Rick.

He says to Five, "You will then be as close to Rick and Latrice as you need be."

Onjito has also been observing from incredible distances away that the Senator is doing some unscrupulous tactics in raising campaign funds.

So from the sinister realm of Onjito, a plan is conjured. Five parts the White Curtain and enters the mystical conduit of the Perimeter, taking himself into the space and exact time of the continuum where Rick and Latrice are. But they are not to be touched and/or harmed.

Onjito made it clear to Five before he departed, "I do not want these pathetic humans interfering with me." If they have no Space Program, they will never be able to detect Onjito's plan for inter-universal domination. Onjito had better be glad that the Creator was allowing for him to have this sort of insight. And Onjito was most assuredly taking advantage of it.

So at the BET Honors at the Warner Center, Senator Jacobs is bent over laughing walking into their posh restroom with a celebrity comedian. All that liquor from the pre and after parties has run quickly through their systems. They both stand at stalls side by side laughing. And there stands what appears to be a somewhat petite man dressed nicely with black slacks, a crisp white formal button down, a black vest, a hand tied bow tie, and a peculiar stylish black hat which casts a shadow over most of his face. Its Five, disguised as a somewhat humble restroom attendant.

He cuts on the water for the gentlemen and first the comedian comes to wash his hands. And he says, "What's up potna? Can I get that mint?"

Five says nothing and mysteriously wipes up any water wasted around his sink. He turns his back to the comedian and arranges his one individualized mint ever so cynically on his black velvet cloth.

"Well, be like that then. That's a dollar I just saved. And you need to cut a light on. A bunch of romantic ass pissin' by your lil' candles from Big Lots. This ain't church." Senator Jacobs laughs while doing his final shake and says, "Talk to you later." And the husky comedian leaves the restroom.

It was not church in this restroom. But the acoustics in this somewhat dark restroom gave the space a spiritual feel. The only light source in the room was at the sink, two small votive candles. The darkness increased starting at the back at the handicap stall and pushed its way up to the urinals onto the mirror and the sink where Five was standing.

The Senator zips his formal slacks up and proceeds to go to the sink where a soft stream of water was already pouring out of the modern designed faucet.

Five says, "Aren't you Senator Jacobs?"

"Yes, I am." The Senator then puts his hands under the water.

Five then gives him one of the venue's monogrammed hand towels.

"Thanks."

Five says, "I just want to congratulate you."

Five takes the towel and shakes his hand. The Senator says, "What is your..." And the Senator's entire body goes numb. His mouth hangs open slightly. He wants to say something or move a part of his body so badly, but the power of Five's touch immobilizes the spine and the entire spinal cord goes dead.

But that is the entire prelude to what is really about to happen. In the Senator's most frightening moment of his life, Five then extracts the Senator's spirit and conscious from his well-dressed physical body. An outer body experience is putting this unexpected display of power very mildly. The physical Senator Jacobs and the spiritual Senator Jacobs, which has a smoke-hazed blue consistency, look at its two confused parts in the mirror.

Five then replaces Senator Ron Jacobs' spirit and conscious with one of his own. It's not Five's spirit per se'. In this state, the Senator will never be the same. Five now has the power over his will to carry out some aspect of his two Masters' plans.

Senator Jacobs' conquered spirit watches in astonishment as sheer evil overtakes his physical body. The empty body takes two short quiet steps in his nice lace-up black Cole Haans. Five walks behind his latest acquisition and smirking in the mirror. Meanwhile, the true spirit of Senator Jacobs does not know what to do. And he becomes even more wide-eyed when Five gives him a piercing look of death, a look that the true Senator Ron Jacobs has never seen before.

And so the true spirit of Senator Ron Jacobs takes off running, trying to grab the door handle but nearly falls back towards his assailant. Senator Ron Jacobs then quickly runs through the door and when he gets the other side he stands in shock of what he is now. Once he gets into the hallway, he starts running down the burgundy carpet and into all kinds of people, mostly sipping their after party cantaloupe martinis. But he runs right through them as well. No one is even able to see Senator Jacobs, and that makes him feel even worse.

Five and Senator Ron Jacobs' physical body both come casually out of the men's room laughing like they were old buddies. Ron's spiritual body watches them both come towards him and gasps, "What have you done to me?"

Five nails him with another kind of contemplative smirk and says, "You can thank me now."

Senator Ron Jacobs' spirit looks back and sees that the portion of the corridor behind Five has morphed into a dark black void. And Senator Ron Jacobs' spirit, in spite of all of his futile efforts, simply gets pulled towards Five and his own physical self. And he tries to grab them but he is unable to. He then gets pulled into the void. This point of entry is dark and its composition is one that strips any virtuous quality of its victim, sending an even weakened spirit to Five's cleverly designed grim holding place.

Five says to him in a quiet voice of jubilation, "Welcome. Forever, welcome."

A tear comes to Five's eye, for he longs for any feeling that strengthens his own decrepit body and soul.

Five has his master Onjito, who looks on from several universes away, to thank for this latest arrival into the Perimeter. It was through his observation that Onjito discovered that funds were originally supposed to be directed to inner city economic development and be used to grease the palms of Congressmen and other Senators to get the support on the Environmental Bill.

Five is confident that he can do an even greater service to this cause by controlling the thoughts and actions of a new Senator Ron Jacobs.

No human being on Earth knew that an alien being was even present.

Ch 11

Rick snaps out of his daze at the Freemason Abbey and sees that Latrice is still trying to reach him via mobile.

Shonnie snatches the phone out of Latrice's hand. "Would you stop calling him if he's not going to pick up. He sees you calling. Just stop it. How far are you going to take this?"

Latrice doesn't want to admit it verbally, but she's thinking, "It's over."

Shonnie adds, "I know it hurts, but girl when it's over you know it is over."

The house was bought in Latrice's name. For the past seven years, she clearly made more money than he did. The furniture belonged to Rick. She loved his taste in decor. He made the house feel like a home. Rick insisted on being a good partner and Latrice allowed him to contribute in whatever honest way that he knew how. His research was fickle and depended on funding from NASA, an agency that was quietly being phased out. Latrice knew this more than anyone.

The recently lost child was symbolic of Rick's contribution to the household as a man. It was utterly important to Rick to have this child considering Latrice, up until this point, was carrying him. And though Latrice made it okay for him to be in his role, there were moments that he hated not working consistently.

Shonnie adds, "And that's okay. That's what marriage is supposed to be about, give and take, even though that mu'fu's taking a lil' more. "

Latrice starts reflecting in an effort to heal her heart. "Rick needed me more than I needed him. I guess I allowed him to think that I needed him just as much. It still doesn't hurt any less. A dump is a dump."

Shonnie chuckles, "Girl you just mad cause he dumped you, and you're wrestling nonstop with the question, "Who the hell is he to be doing that to you?"

And the first chuckle erupts from Latrice. "He's gonna go back to his mother and get what he needs."

Shonnie adds, "And them Facebook women." And the smile on Latrice's face disappears. Shonnie notices, "What? Oh you better not give me that face. You know good and well Rick is going to cling onto one of them women to get a hot meal. But like my grand momma says, 'He knows where his meat and bread is.'"

Latrice knew that he really wasn't that kind of guy. She says to Shonnie, "I wish you'd just be quiet."

They find a way to produce happiness in their joint moment of sadness. Latrice nods her head, "I guess it's over."

One week has passed, and there has been no way that Latrice has been able to escape thinking about Rick. Come on. The woman has needs. And her needs are directly connected to what Rick has to offer. The length of days and long life and peace that Latrice has been missing has caused her to relish in the recklessness of her misguided thoughts of lust. So dear Latrice finds herself at the steps of Rick's new apartment in Newport News.

"Can we talk?"

Rick stands at the front door, "You're doing it again."

She responds, "What? I'm doing what? You're just going to let me stand out here?"

Ch 12

Early the next morning, Shonnie's cell phone rings and she knows who it is. "Girl, what's up?"

Latrice is driving home and says, "I just wanted to let you know I just saw Rick."

Shonnie is in the kitchen warming up a cup of tea, "Mm hmm. I know. Couldn't stay away from him could you?"

Latrice, feeling judged by her girl, makes a left turn onto her street and pulls up in the drive way. "Girl I ain't going back over there again. It's over. You know I found a pack of condemns in his wallet when he went to the bathroom."

Shonnie says, "You still ain't learned your lesson have you? I can't believe you."

Latrice interjects, "Girl I ain't lettin' him stick his penis in me and he's around here… doing I don't know what!"

But Latrice knows that all that is a lie. She is the last person who wants to roll around in that big bed of theirs without his wonderful thighs and arms holding her and keeping her warm. Just thinking about Rick's absence makes Latrice yearn for his lips on the back of her neck, not to mention any feelings of validation connected to their penis that she seems so eager to dismiss.

Shonnie shakes her head and says, "Then why are you still chasing him?"

Latrice bashfully responds, "Because I need some dick."

Shonnie shakes her head in disbelief. "Then go and get a new one. There's a bunch of em' out there. And to be honest, some of them are attached to some pretty decent people."

Latrice gets home and goes into her seemingly abandoned house. "I'm sick of you and all this untried advice of yours. What newness have you stumbled upon lately?"

And a six foot five hunk of a ball player has come over. He's quietly walking up on Shonnie, squeezing her butt as he intentionally interrupts the whole flow of the conversation. Latrice hears a quiet deep voice on her end of the phone and then a bunch of kissing. Latrice says, "Hello?"

Shonnie is being pulled over to a chair in the dining room. "Girl, so what are you about to do? Are you okay?"

Shonnie gets a little nervous as she anticipates what this big ole' dude is about to do. On the other end, Latrice just listens. She can hear the clothes coming off, the bra being undone as Shonnie is about to get some for herself. She says to Latrice in a breathier voice, "You still there girl?"

And in a matter of seconds, the man in Shonnie's presence has her turned around, so that she can bounce the rest of the morning away to her delight. But Shonnie is so much of a good friend that she doesn't know how to hang up with Latrice. And Latrice is not trying to hear all of that. "Bye. Call me later hoe. Bye."

Shonnie is simply in her own little piece of deserved heaven. "Later Hoe. Bye." She makes no sense. But her loyalty is what is needed in this moment. Shonnie is the key to comfort. Without her,

Latrice is left to put the pieces together for herself. Can she trust herself to talk her way through her issues?

"Why do we need to be apart? Doesn't he love me the way I need to be loved? Who is the fault? Why does anyone need to be blamed? Should I have a better option of men?   Can I have the happiness that I deserve? Have I done all that I was supposed to do to keep him? Was I too needy? I'm cold. I need him. I can't force him to be with me. But I can't help the way I feel. I need him. But outside of this one person, should my needs fall to someone else to mold? How can we disconnect? Who can rescue me? I did everything that I was supposed to do.... I think. I don't know. I remember how this feeling came to visit me. And it so does not feel good. It's a pirate... there to steel all of my joy... all of my peace... and then my piece of mind. I love what I can't have when what I have can't seem to give me... oh I'm not making any sense. I just want to go somewhere and have someone to love me the way I need love. But I keep... I want to be kept... so I dig deep and promise that I will keep him... so that I can be kept in his thoughts. Just keep me in mind. Think of me. I just want you to love me. But you don't want to. So I'll take myself and hide. And then I'll have to hate you... for not being able to help me with my heart and the heaviness of what I cannot explain about myself. I love myself, but I want you to love me more so that I can be in awe of the margin of what I am missing. Let me love you... so that I can love me. I'll be in so much... I don't know what I'm saying. So I'll stop. I guess I can say my good-byes at this point. It hurts." These pure and unfiltered thoughts provide the cadence for Latrice to handwrite a very heartfelt letter while in the frontseat of her sports car. She drops this letter in the mail to Rickland. Signed, *"Love, Latrice."*

Since the Creator set forth these stern rules of engagement, Onjito has been studying every facet of Rick and Latrice's lives. He understood that if Rick was somehow hindered in terms of his ability to provide and procreate, then Latrice's spirit would begin to slowly decay. He sees, through their integrated lives, that Senator Ron Jacobs and Rick have a love and hate relationship brewing, all around this woman named Latrice.

Onjito made it clear to Five, "I do not want these pathetic humans interfering in my affairs." If they have no Space Program, they will never be able to detect his plan for trans-universal domination.

Ch 13

Ron Jacobs, now referred to as RJ-5 by his maker, is caught running up the steps of the US Capitol in DC where he will meet with the Committee on Space and Technology to vote on whether to approve funds in order to begin research.

Though he is on the other side of the Perimeter, anxiously attempting to cross over to this universe's timeline, Lord Onjito wants to put an end to space exploration on Earth. He still has strings tied to Five and is able to manipulate RJ-5 (Senator Ron Jacobs) to utilize his political power to achieve this goal. And since the Senator sits on the Senate Space and Environment Subcommittees, it would be relatively easy to shut US space exploration down completely.

Once RJ-5 gets settled in his own office, he goes over to Senator Dick Lightsy's office, Senate Subcommittee Chair for the Environment, and begins negotiating on how to appropriate funds. RJ-5 proposes, "Rob I need your help in pulling back funding for defense satellite development. All of this talk about the possibility of an alien invasion. Give me a break! Who started us down this path?" And he laughs while sitting on the edge of a table in Senator Lightsy's office.

Lightsy reclines back in his office and lights up one of his many rare and expensive Cuban cigars. "So Ron what are you proposing? I know whatever it is, it's gonna cost me something."

RJ-5 says nothing but the plan rest heavily in his face.

Two days later, Rick gets a knock on the door. He's dressed in a t-shirt, jeans, and socks as he walks across the hardwood floors of the foyer of his new apartment. He looks through the door and it's RJ-5. Rick says, "What do you want?"

RJ-5 responds, "Hey chill. I just wanted to have a word with you."

Rick still hasn't let him in. "How did you know..." And then he catches himself. He remembers that he's a Senator. And two of his Secret Service Detail are in the driveway making sure that Rick keeps a level head. One is Caucasian and locks eyes with Rick as if to say, "Give me the excuse to put one right between your pretty eyes."

RJ-5 sees the connection and says, "That's a big guy, huh?"

Rick responds, "What do you want?"

"May I come in?"

And RJ-5 does. He wipes his feet on the charcoal grey mat and comes in. "Nice place. How long…"

Rick doesn't feel like answering any of his questions, "Look, I said…"

"All right. All right. I have something I'd like to talk to you about. I know that you are looking, seeking for something."

"And?"

RJ-5 responds, "And I would like to help you in your discovery process."

Rick folds his arms, signaling that he's on the defensive and his face tenses up.

RJ-5 says, "Listen. Relax. I'm not going to bite you."

Rick can only think of the somewhat settled friction of yesteryear between the two of them over Latrice.

RJ-5 says, "All that stuff is over, as far I'm concerned. I know that Latrice and you have been going through a lot. I want to get you a better career over at NASA. I was just speaking with Senator Dick Lightsy, who chairs…"

"I know. I know, the Subcommittee on the Environment within Space and Technology."

RJ-5 continues, "Well we think that we'd like to have a study done on the effects of global warming on our atmosphere."

Rick responds, "So where are you sending me, to Florida?"

RJ-5 says, "Eventually yes, but I was thinking you could continue to stay here locally and do this."

"And what exactly is this?"

"I have a better equipped lab all prepared for you over in Hampton at Langley."

Rick responds, "What is this really about?"

"I need research. You need a job."

"More like, you need money and you need me to give it to you."

They're still not too far from the front door. Rick really doesn't want him in the house.

RJ-5 responds, "I can easily get whoever to do this. I just figured that with you and Latrice suffering a miscarriage..."

Rick interjects, "And then what the hell was that about you getting her fired? So you're gonna come over here now and offer me a job just so you can snatch that away too?"

RJ-5 says, "Listen. I get it."

"No you don't."

"Yes I do. That lobbying effort is getting phased out. Latrice, Susan, everyone is gonna get the ax over there at some point. What this is is off the radar, which means you have a lot of latitude, within reason, to produce the results that the committee is ultimately looking for."

The wheels in Rick's head cannot help but to turn. "I'll think about it."

RJ-5 says, "You've already thought about it. Here is your brand new security clearance, which was not that difficult to get, considering your uh couple recent hits, dings on your credit report."

RJ-5 pulls out the credential and hands it over to Rick. Rick kind of snatches it from RJ-5.

"Stay out of my records."

"Pay your student loans. Now I owe the Education Secretary a favor because of you."

Rick looks at the clear and transparent card. "What's this? There's nothing on it?

RJ-5 responds, "Hold it out, with your thumb."

And Rick does. RJ-5 takes an infrared light beam out of his inside pocket of his pen-striped suit and scans it back and forth over the clear card. Rick sees a faint image of his face with a barcode over top of it in the left hand corner.

Rick says, "I don't need this. My lab over at Hampton University will do just fine."

RJ-5 responds, "Don't take this the wrong way, but... we can't do what we need to do with you in that environment."

Rick responds, "Why not?"

"Because we just can't." RJ-5 was getting a little uncomfortable and he wasn't going to budge from this. His body language was making Rick uncomfortable.

RJ-5 continues, "Ahh, you need to think of your perception a little more."

That jolts Rick, "What does that mean?"

RJ-5 says, "I am just saying that when you're dealing in very sophisticated endeavors, you have to watch who is surrounding you."

Rick squints his eyes and offers a slight smile and says, "Oh you mean so many Black people. Right. Right. Right."

RJ-5 says, "I'm gonna set you up over at Langley... top of the line, state of the art facility, all available for you to do your best work. And that's what the hell I want. And that's what the committee needs."

RJ-5 puts his shades on and opens the well-sealed front door. As he heads down the brick steps and walks down the curvy sidewalk, and into his silver GMC sport utility vehicle. The Secret Service Detail makes sure he's secure and they make a U-turn out of the complex.

Rick looks out the window through the white miniblinds and breathes heavy.

Later on that afternoon, Rick goes over to Uncle Smitty's house in Portsmouth. Its Rick's favorite uncle. He's cool as all get out. Smitty has the smile of Teddy P. with the swag of Frankie Beverly.

Rick makes his way down the Hatton Point Lane where it dead ends in a beautiful subdivision where Uncle Smitty owns a nice modest two-story brick home, sitting right on the Elizabeth River. Rick likes going over there to enjoy the sun setting behind the ships on the water in West Norfolk. But he's early. He's got about a couple hours of day light left. He comes in and sees one of Smitty's latest dime-pieces walking around in tight dark denim jeans and a navy blue wife-beater.

She opens the door and only thing that's nice than her eyes, hair, and smile is the path that the white stitching makes along her nice thighs, hips, and tiny waist. And then the smell of Italian cooking from the kitchen hits his nose.

Smitty did that on purpose. He likes to show off his thick women to Rick when he comes over.

She says, "He's out back."

Rick walks out back and steps out onto the concrete patio. He easily slides the glass door shut to keep all the cool air inside. He looks out into the distant and there's Smitty, standing out on the dark wood pier that goes out 30 yards over the calmness of the river.

Smitty looks over his back and sees the essence of him and his deceased brother, Rickland Foster. "There he is. What's up there boy?"

Smitty hugs his nephew and he can sense that there is heaviness on him. And reacts in such a way that he releases the hug a second too soon. He says to Rick, "Rick, watch your feet now. I noticed a couple of nails sticking up when I walked out here. I might need for you to help me before you leave."

Rick responds, "Cool." And he just stands there and looks out over the river like he's always done.

Smitty says, "You doin' all right?"

"I'm good."

Smitty responds, "How's Latrice, you know... since that... happened.?

Rick nods his head repeatedly and says nothing. And lips get a little tight. His eyes begin to flicker and they produce instant tears. The very thought of what he's lost produces a toughness in his tender throat that prevents Rick from speaking.

Smitty puts his beer down on the table and opens his arms. "I'm sorry man. I am so sorry."

Kathy is inside washing lettuce at the sink and she sees a side of Smitty that's she's never seen before, he and his nephew bonding. She smiles and feels so happy for him because Smitty does not have any children of his own.

Smitty has a way of comforting you if he likes you. And for him, there was no other man that he wanted to see happy than his nephew Rick.

Smitty says, "I mean you know. I know I rubbed off on you somehow. You may be Mr. NASA, schmoozing with the big dogs on Capitol Hill, but me and your daddy raised you... to be a man."

Talking about his accomplishments was Smitty's way of getting through uncomfortable moments. And since they were standing on a prize piece of Tidewater property, Smitty's emotions escaped from the moment. And he picks up his beer and he pulls the brim of his baby blue Kangol down a little bit. Smitty takes his brown tinted shades off.

"You know I'ma always have the finest. I don't care if you talkn' bout cars, clothes, or these hoes, you know your uncle's gonna have the baddest."

Rick says, "What ever happened to that 84' Cutlass that you had?"

Just before Smitty answers that, Kathy comes out with her extra fine self and starts setting the patio table.

Smitty responds, "I still got it. Er'body used to be all over that car." Rick sees Smitty's eyes all on Kathy. Smitty adds, "Er' car ain't worth keepin'. But that right there? That's a classic." Kathy knows he's talking about her. And she makes a quick funny face and sashays back in the house.

And then something strange was happening to Rick. He was feeling unusually aware of everything around him. He turns around and off in the distant he sees older white folks coming out to see what was going on. They were obviously not that used to people like Smitty living near them. The soft bass from Smitty's stereo on the patio bumping Maze's Golden Time of Day might have had something to do with that.

Rick gazes into the calm and wide Elizabeth River and uses it as a beautiful screen in which to see that which his father's brother remembers.

Smitty says, "Let me tell you something Rick. You live where you want to live. Work where you want to work. I've been at the Shipyard for over 20 years." Rick sees Smitty remembering himself in 1984 driving his brother in his new Cutlass over the long James River Bridge.

Smitty continues, "Stop following white people around. When I was young back in the 60's, won't nothin' but white people living out here in Churchland. Then they saw us coming and they started moving all the way out to the Oceanfront. What they didn't ask themselves was 'When I get to the Atlantic, where do I go next? Where do I go after I move to the ocean?' Back to where you were. You see what I'm saying? So stop followin' nem motherfu'. Oops, I ain't supposed to be cussin'."

Kathy might have heard that. She looks out the patio window and sees him smiling at her.

Smitty says to Rick in a now raspy voice, "Girl got Smitty going to church. Jesus shole nuff bout to come back now."

Smitty is the King of his world standing out on his pier, arms stretch out with a beer in one hand, and not caring about the slightly disgruntled elderly neighbors looking at him.

Smitty continues, "My point is, don't be ashamed of living around your own people."

Rick asks, "Well where are your black neighbors?"

As Smitty swallows another sip of his brew, he says, "I'm looking at her."

Rick turns his head and its Kathy. She's been leaning up against a post for a about five minutes.

"Y'all ready?"

Rick thinks back on what RJ-5 told him earlier. And he says to his uncle who's throwing his bottle in a baby blue disposable trash bag, "Thanks. I needed to hear that."

The sun rests on the Elizabeth River, and all three walk back towards the house to eat dinner on Smitty's laid patio.

Rick hasn't stopped thinking of Latrice and his daughter. But he takes in how Smitty and Kathy seem to fit together so well. It's so beautiful to him. The closeness of their chairs makes it obvious that they want to be together. A glimmer of the lights begin the sparkle from the safety and security of still navy vessels both far away and near. Smitty's brick riverside home, located between the Churchland and West Norfolk Bridges, is indeed this man's castle. Smitty touches Kathy's pretty red-bone ring finger while at the table, and rubs it in a circular motion, as if something was there. She understands him, and she touches his face ever so tenderly. There's no need for her to say anything. Her eyes say it all. A gentle breeze blows through Kathy's hair, exposing a part of her forehead that Smitty really admires and finds attractive. But they can't carry on like they want to because Rick is there.

Rick says, "Unc', I'm a go ahead and wrap this up to go. I got a long day tomorrow."

Smitty walks him to the door, and they hug, reminiscent of a father and son. Smitty gives Rick all that he occasionally misses, which is quite often.

And Rick accidentally makes a left onto High Street towards Norfolk. But he suddenly remembers that he's not going home to Latrice. He makes a U-turn right before the Churchland Bridge and takes the long way down Route 17, over the James River Bridge to Hampton. On the passenger seat of his white 66' Mercury Cougar, he sees the letter that he's afraid to read from Latrice. Sometimes he wishes that his life was as simple as Smitty's.

Once he gets over the four and half mile bridge, Rick makes a right turn and pulls over to read the letter. He gives up no emotion or indication as to whether he really cares. But that's Rick. It's almost intentional. Like this was his way of showing that he was superior.

Latrice was preparing for bed, scarfing up her hair, brushing her teeth, getting into a lonely bed for two, and cutting out her light. The words of her letter are her last thoughts for the night.

She could hear the sounds of the pages in Rick's beautiful strong hands, how his eyes looked as they read across the page, and how often he'd have to look away to gather his thoughts. Latrice was hoping that each word would be taken in the fashion that it was given. Her hopeful eyes made heaven out of her tall crowned molded ceiling as her soft cheek rested peacefully on a very cold pillow. It was an indication that Latrice really longed for their hearts to somehow be reconnected.

CH 14

A couple of days have passed, and by Latrice writing that letter to Rick, it exhausted her and taxed her emotions. She was sitting in a very quiet house, doing nothing with herself, and trying to figure out what the hell had become of her life. "I have no job, no husband, and..." Her eyes flutter rapidly as the hardest thought to accept impedes her ability to swallow her recent and greatest loss ever. And so instead of allowing these thoughts to overtake her, Latrice takes the pillows off the bed and hurls them everywhere. She then hops out of their high bed, opens the blinds, gets into the shower, and prepares herself for some major piddling around the house.

Latrice is trying to muster up the confidence to stand bold and not let this circumstance claim her spirit completely. But this evil agenda was already prepared by Five, long before this day.

So Latrice puts on some tight but very comfortable grey sweats that stop just below her knee, and then those bright neon-orange colored sneakers, and then she rushes down the two flights of stairs into the dark empty two car garage. The oil spot on Rick's side wasn't fresh, signally that his car hasn't been in the garage, but she knew that and she thinks, "Oh well, whatever."

She's got a huge stash of DVD's that she's been looking at forever. Most of the movies are corny and he doesn't look at anyway. Besides, if they were that important, he would have taken them with him.

Her cell phone rings and its Shonnie. "What's up? Whatcha doin'?"

Latrice is sifting through DVD's. "Not a whole lot. You know a sister gotta go back to eatin' noodles since she ain't got no job." They laugh.

"I know that's right."

Latrice is trying to keep some of her favorite movies. "Nah, I'm just going through these DVD's, trying to decide what to keep and what to sell. I'm just gonna sell all his stuff."

And just like that, Latrice is quickly walking out of her garage with three big red Macy's bags of DVD's and getting into the car. "So how was your '8th wonder of the world'?"

Shonnie is washing dishes, "Oh you mean Mr. Wonderful, just as fine as he wants to be."

Latrice is driving and is about to get onto the freeway and merges into the middle lane. "You don't even know his name."

Shonnie is looking at herself in the mirror admiring her voluptuous curves. "Yes I do. His username is Mr. Wonderful".

And Latrice almost has an accident. "Hold up. His username? What the... who in the hello is Mr. Wonderful? Shonnie where did you meet him this man?"

Shonnie sits down at her well decorated circular dining room table. "I feel like talking to my mother."

Latrice breaks the law and snatches her headset off so she can hear. "Spill it! Or should I say, bend it?"

Shonnie hits the repeat button on the new Miguel song that was playing as her limbs were getting bent back. She gets back in front of the mirror and does the freaky dance that led to last night's excursion. She can still feel his rhythm in the room. "Girl he brought all of that specialness up in here yesterday and just blessed me so. I really have nothing to say."

Latrice responds, "Really."

"Mm, hmm. Really."

Latrice is in the car moving at least 80 miles an hour and not paying attention to the road. "Well goodness, what did he do?"

And Shonnie sighs. "Girl, what didn't he do? Okay first off we've been talking for about six months."

Latrice's mouth drops. "You hoe! What?"

Shonnie laughs, "Yes, you know I don't be lettin' strange men know where I live."

Latrice rolls her eyes up in her head. "Sure." And she gets in the left lane and that pretty lil' led foot goes to work.

"So he flew in from New York. He's an attorney and he had to represent a client in Norfolk. So I picked him up from the airport, and girl when those big ole' legs and shoulders got up in my car! Girl shoot!

Hisbuttwas looking at relocating as far as I was concerned."

Latrice is smiling from ear to ear. "Ok, well you know the real question is what did he think of you?"

Shonnie sits in her talking chair. "Well, first off I had his complete and undivided attention. He was coming to see all this momma that he was loving in all these photos."

Latrice gets off at the Brambleton Exit. "Momma?"

Shonnie is eating some left over fruit from last night. "I absolutely love it when he calls me that. You know, it's a term of endearment. Whenever he says that to me we go into a place of intimacy that is so powerful, I cannot even begin to describe. It is so special."

Latrice pulls up into the parking garage. "Hold up. Stop right there. I want to hear more but I gotta take these DVD's inside to sell."

Shonnie went to her bedroom and is on her knees by the bed trying to smell the sheets.

Latrice hears her. "What are you doing? I know you're not trying to smell the sheets.

But in an attempt to relive last night, that's exactly what Shonnie was doing.

Shonnie is still on her knees. "Be quiet. He's here til tomorrow. What you need to do is go onto www.meetmyking.net and fill out a dating profile."

Latrice is out of the car and is on foot. "What! Meet my who?"

Shonnie laughs. "Don't laugh. And they do their own screening for you."

Even if she wasn't dealing with Rick, everybody isn't for Latrice. Latrice suffers from what most women suffer from, a bunch of men staring and no balls to step to her. Already, she's walked by three guys pretending to be shopping but they're all silently checking her out.

The workers who are supposed to be stocking and restocking cannot help but to stare. The spell that Latrice can put on a guy is just wonderful, dangerous without even trying.

After the owner of the used record shop peruses through the several bags of DVD's at the counter, Latrice walks away with a whole 14 dollars. This strange mysterious owner, who is about seven months pregnant, asks Latrice, "We're doing a special promo. If you sign up for a dating profile on MeetMyKing.net we will take 20 percent off your next purchase. I'll even give you your first month free."

Latrice is in no mood for fussing, but conversely she's receptive and needs healing through the niceness and kindness of others. And this is the second time that this website has been introduced to her, in less than 30 minutes. Latrice says, "Sure, I'll check it out."

The store owner's name is Kaylandria, and she rips off her receipt. "So actually what you can do is go over to the coffee shop, log on to one of the computers and you can set up your profile. And if you have problems, someone can help you with it."

Latrice didn't hear a word she just said. She can't take her eyes off of Kaylandria's baby bump. It's as if her own remaining life was inside of her.

Kaylandria says, "Ma'am. Ma'am." And Latrice snaps out of her daze.

Kaylandria says, "Your receipt."

Latrice pulls herself together. "Oh yeah… thanks."

She's sick of this unwanted feeling hammering her. "How much more can I honestly take? Leave me alone." But the strength of Latrice's curiosity kicks in to gear. And she takes a stroll through the length of the store and wonders over to the coffee shop.

The Creator's timing is everything. None of the customers want to get up from their seat. A short little elderly woman with a hair bun, glasses, classic hosiery, skinny ankles, and flats is getting ready to leave and signals Latrice, "Come. I'm about to leave. You can have this station."

And Latrice comes over and sits down. "Thank you."

The mother type is just wrapping up. "Oh, no worries honey. Just checking to see if I had any men checking in on me."

Latrice wants to chuckle, "Are you on Meet My…?"

She interjects, "I got me some Kings trying to holla!"

Oh Latrice just wants to crack up. She reminds her of her late grandmother.

"Enjoy." She leaves.

The ergonomic computer station is on a swivel table. Latrice turns it around and she sees a couple walk behind her and she sees it in the reflection of the monitor. Latrice turns around to admire. And even though her mind is still on Rick... she needs to be reconnected with someone who is growing. "How do I miss someone and still move forward, without seeming like I'm desperate and on the rebound?"

Kaylandria taps Latrice on her shoulder and she turns around. "You're going to miss him for a while, but in time, in the right time, your heart will heal. So just enjoy your life. Don't rush. Start off with listening to his thoughts. And then invite the thoughts that you like into your own space."

Latrice sighs and smiles, "I don't know how you knew that, but that is exactly what I needed to hear. Thank you."

And then Latrice, shuts her eyes, and tunes out every sound around her. And she surrenders to her need. Her inner voice says, *"Let go."*

Cʜ 15

That same morning, Rick wakes up at the break of dawn on his mattress and box spring, and has a revelation. "Yeah."

Far, far away in the heavens, in His inner chambers, the Creator was whispering directly to Rick, "Find me."

Rick makes himself a cup of coffee, the best he can, and finds his way over to his own lab space at Hampton University. He starts out examining the atmosphere of his home Earth. But he asks himself, "Where are the dots that need to be connected?" But he gets frustrated because he has no idea what the dots are. He sits and rubs his head frantically, searching for the answers.

Rick doesn't know who or what, but he hears the voice of the Creator. And he hears the words, "Instead of looking and thinking out, look from within." They're words that he's always heard all of his life, his tall jolly 4th grade science teacher Mr. Sarris, his deceased parents, and even Latrice would say some version of it. They encouraged him to search his inner man to find the answer. Rick really didn't know the extent to which those words had taken root. And then his heart begins to beat faster, and louder, and stronger, until he thinks of the loss of his angelic daughter, an agonizing thought that he has had to accept and bear its weight. Rick sits on his normal lab stool and gets stuck in his thoughts.

Rick can feel the blood pulsating and moving throughout the veins in his arms, legs, back, and head. He hears Uncle Smitty's voice from yesterday on the pier, "We gotta live in the moment."

So, Rick decides to do something crazy and take a chance. He does blood work on himself. He draws the blood and then properly stores it at the right temperature. Rick then begins to theorize an untested algorithm out on his favorite portable flipping chalk boards. One side of the board attempted to draw a theorized equation on the universe, and on the other side, he drew another algorithm on evolution and sustainability of a basic human cell.

Realizing how the greatest minds in science including Newton and Einstein have always influenced him, a relatively unknown African American from Virginia was inspired this day by his recent loss and by the quiet whispers into his spirit by the Creator. Rickland worked as if he had lost something precious that he found some time ago, but never got a chance to fully embrace it.

Cн 16

Meanwhile, many light years away and nestled in a remote part of a peculiar universe, the ruthless ruler Onjito looks on from afar utter disapproval and he knows that there is nothing that he can do about Rick's inspired progress.

The Creator had provided a boundary of protection around Rick, of course unbeknownst to him, in order for him to deal with the pain of the loss of his child and find a way to channel it. "I told you. Neither one of them are to be touched or harmed."

Though sleepless nights and being inspired in the manner in which he was, Rick's theorized findings were now ready to be put back into the bloodstream by way of a complex engineered nutrient. He murmurs, "If life is a function of time, and cells are the rudimentary basic building block of life. Then it would stand to reason that the creation of cells is dependent on... time. It's all a matter of time." And next he begins to think about the concept of time and how humans deal with it.

Later on that night in his new temporary home, Rick writes in his journal, "We know how to record time as a measurement. But do we really know what time is? Does time live? How else could life sustain itself over time if time was not a function of life as well?" And Rick has an ah-ha moment and says, "Codependent. Time and Life are functions of each other, making them interdependent!"

He places his fingers on his temple while sitting at his cluttered home desk. He's neglected the upkeep of what is now home for him. Sofa cushions and pillows are all over the floor and the hallway leading to the kitchen. Spending nights on the floor, working out different pieces of these equations in random places in the house, Rick is completely letting his appearance go. In seven days, he had bathed once. His breath stinks. Rick hadn't changed his underwear in days. This was a man who was travelling from passion to inspiration to deep places of depression, all caused by his recent losses, Latrice and his daughter.

For the sake of responsibility and confidentiality, Rick decided to use himself as the one and only test subject. This was nowhere near what the Senate Committee on Space and Technology was paying him to do. But it was what was truly resonating in his heart.

So Rick pushes up the sleeves of his thermal long sleeve and injects the nutrient directly into the fattest vein in his forearm. He tosses the syringe onto the lab counter and makes a fist and bends his left arm back and forth. He has no clue what to expect.

If his calculations to his theory are correct, and if Rick's immune system does not automatically catch what it perceives to be a harmful foreign substance, then Rick's molecular cell structure will rewrite his specific biological time signature on just one cell.

One cell is all that he needs. Once one reacts to the nutrient, then it can be tracked.

If there was only one thing that could be proven in this exercise was that the work on the Space program must not come to a halt. He'll deal with Ron Jacobs and the Senate Subcommittee on Science and Space the best way he can. Hopefully, there will be astounding results that will make for more serious and honest debates about the universe, life, and time.

The problem is that Rick had no proven way of tracking the action and making quick enough and more importantly informed enough decisions to keep the test on track, really knowing where he will go, or even more to the point, how it will alter him.

Rick stares straight ahead, wide eyed, as he takes the nutrient in the privacy of his lab. He waits a decent about of time and he doesn't feel any different.

But little did he know that his body was indeed changing, quietly but dramatically. The labor of Rick's work, every variable, every equation, was taking root in the code of his DNA. But Rick could not feel the change and as a result he became very frustrated.

In the overall scheme at work, Rick was being played to the nth degree by Five, who was plotting to use this breakthrough for him and his master Onjito's strategic advantage.

But the Creator and in his infinite wisdom knew of this plan as well, and had already decided that it would be proper to intervene.

The Creator would conceal the progress of the divinely inspired engineered nutrient within his body as it now quietly travels throughout Rick's bloodstream.

CH 17

A week has gone by since Latrice met Kaylandria. She runs into Latrice while at the local farmer's market in the beautiful Ghent section near downtown Norfolk. And they begin walking enjoying the day together. She says to Latrice, "You know, destiny is a funny thing. Sometimes you control it, sometimes you can't. Sometimes destiny really helps you to discover not just where you're going, but the manner in which you arrive."

It's a beautiful day. Latrice doesn't know where that statement came from, but she's feeling too vulnerable to allow this conversation to go too deep. "How often do you come here?"

The sweet elderly Kaylandria says, "Oh, I've been coming here for a long time... long time."

They stop by the strawberry tent and Latrice asks, "Ok, what I am dying to know…"

Kaylandria responds, "Yeah, come on. Spit it out."

Latrice tries to muster up some boldness and says, "How…?"

"How can I be so old and carrying a baby?"

Latrice opens up and responds, "Well, yeah!"

"If you live as old as me, maybe you'll find out."

They wrap up their shopping. But suddenly Kaylandria drops her bag of fruit and a key onto the street.

Latrice catches her, "Are you okay?" Latrice quickly goes down to gather Kaylandria's fresh peaches and lettuce and notices the key.

Kaylandria says, "Just hold onto that for me please."

"What is it?"

"Just an extra key to the house. That thing will get lost in my purse if I don't hold it." She almost hurt herself. Kaylandria loses her balance sometimes.

Latrice says, "Okay. Do you need a ride home?"

"Oh, would you please?"

"Of course."

Latrice gets Kaylandria into the sports car. But she drives extra slow and thinks, "Stupid Rick, this is how he should have been driving me."

Kaylandria holds her head and has her eyes closed as she tries to catch her breath. Latrice is really concerned for her.

Latrice says, "Kaylandria, I'm going to take you to Norfolk General, okay?"

"No."

"Why not?"

"I don't want to go there."

"But the hospital is just right around the corner."

"Please... just take me home."

"Okay... but."

"I'm about ten minutes away."

Latrice does not have a good feeling about this and doesn't feel like going to any strange house. And besides she doesn't know her. But she takes her down Brambleton Avenue. There are just so many stoplights to make anyone annoyed and on edge. A black man with a scruffy beard, baseball cap, worn down shoes, pushing a shopping cart comes up alongside the car while at the light.

He says, "Ma'am, can I do your windows?"

Latrice says, "Uh no. I don't have time for this."

Kaylandria says, "Here, give him this, even though he might be up to something." Kaylandria gives Latrice a twenty dollar bill. Latrice gives it to the man. The light changes, and they take off. The man stands there with a curious look on his face.

Kaylandria says, "You're going to 1817 Montclair."

They leave the certain poshness of Ghent and go by Tidewater Park, then the ABC Store, and over the

Campostella Bridge. There's always been a slight stench of petroleum oil that one could smell when they hit the metal grid at the top. Latrice hates riding over the that metal grid, and is happy that today is a not a day that a ship needs to come through.

She comes off the bridge at the right time of day and smells seasoned fried crabs all the way up the street from Eddie's as she sits at the light waiting to turn. Latrice takes Kaylandria to her home. It's a very tall, whimsical Victorian home near another portion of the Elizabeth River.

Kaylandria is pregnant indeed. Her breathing, moaning, discomfort, everything suggests that she is going into labor. Latrice looks and she has to admit to herself, "I don't want any parts of this."

This is no ordinary pregnancy.

"Help me upstairs."

"I don't think that's such a good idea."

"Trust me."

"If you just sit here…"

"I want to go upstairs."

Kaylandria knew it, and Latrice was starting to believe that she belonged upstairs. She opens the door and Latrice helps Kaylandria to walk very gingerly up the long rich dark chestnut stairway. The stairs have a slight creek to them, but Latrice is more so concerned about making sure that Kaylandria's foot lands on every step. But not to worry, the banister that they both clutch to gives assistance. Latrice observes the rail is actually helping them both upstairs, pulling them along the way, like an escalator rail, but more organic, more fluid.

And then the steps actually bring them upstairs, and Latrice no longer has to struggle with bringing her upstairs. Everything is being done by elements of the house as if it had something prepared.

Latrice feels out of place and she asks the question to herself, "Well what did she need me for?" They get to the top of the steps and land on Kaylandria's beautiful afghan rug. Latrice has no clue where to go. Kaylandria's breathing prevents her from uttering any sentence that makes any sense. So the beautiful rug stretches itself around to the second floor railing to the left somehow and makes a winding path as to where they should go. With most of Kaylandria's weight on Latrice, she takes one step forward. And the elongated rug takes them into the second room. The five other doors remain shut. There are six rooms in all on this strange second floor.

Latrice lays Kaylandria on her bed.

"Listen, I'm going to call a paramedic. We need help."

Kaylandria replies, "Sit here next to me."

Latrice sits on the area inside the bay window. She looks outside and sees a little girl staring up at her standing in the middle of the street. The little girl sees directly into her Latrice with a dark stare. Latrice breaks eye contact.

With no hesitation, Kaylandria has broken out into a fever.

"Oh my goodness. You are sweating."

"It's what happens when you're pregnant."

That didn't sit too well with Latrice. That sends Latrice back to a not so happy place with her own pregnancy.

She helps her out of her clothes.

"Look over there in that drawer… on the left hand side. It should be right there on top."

All of the furniture is rather dated but in great shape, late 19th century.

Latrice brings the clothes over to Kaylandria. And they slowly but surely work off one set of clothes to get on another.

"Whew, much better. I can't stand having all them clothes on me."

Latrice smiles.

Kaylandria says, "You are one beautiful woman."

"Thank you, but you need someone else other than me. Who is your doctor?"

"Trust me, there is no doctor who specializes in what's about to happen."

And all of sudden, Kaylandria goes into labor.

She screams, "Uhhhhhhh!!!"

Latrice gets one of the white rags and runs to the bathroom to wet it.

"Come back here!"

She drops the rag and leaves the bathroom water running.

Latrice gets up and starts pacing the floor. Her arms are folded. And then she jumps over to the front of the bed.

"Kaylandria, okay I want you to push when I say push… not a moment before."

"Don't tell me what to do. I know what to do."

"Okay. I'm sorry. I'm just trying to help."

"Latrice."

"Yes."

"Come over here and hold my hand and don't say a word."

"Okay."

And Latrice does just that. She comes over to her and sits still... saying nothing... holding Kaylandria's hand.

"Uhhhhhhh!!!"

The closeness to this sound of anguish sends Latrice to her knees while holding her hand.

And all of a sudden, the room, the house, the street, the city of Norfolk, the state of Virginia, the United States, North America, and then the Earth, everything on the planet goes black for seven seconds. And then there is light. But Latrice notices that there is no Kaylandria.

Latrice gets up and looks everywhere for her. She sticks her head out into the hallway, she sees nothing. She quickly comes back in the bathroom and cuts the water off, and then walks back into the bedroom.

There stands a strange man. And it startles Latrice. Then she looks, and it's the same homeless man that was begging in the street just a few minutes ago. But he has on a very strange long formed rather fitted black suit, or maybe it was just his appearance that made any suit look strange.

Latrice sticks close to the wall and knocks a framed picture off that wall and she falls to the floor.

Leaning down into Latrice's face with his long rectangular face, he says, "I am sorry. Please do not be startled."

He goes over to help Latrice up.

"What is going on? Who are you?" Latrice says.

He refers to what is now an empty bed, all nice and neat, with a hand knitted white spread, "What you just witnessed was a birth."

Latrice stays clinging to the wall with her eyes trying to look at the bed, but this dark man with an age that has no number is just way too eerie to ignore. "What did you do with her?"

"I did nothing with her."

"I am not playing with you. Let me go."

"I am afraid that you cannot leave just yet."

"I am leaving right now."

Latrice tries to go for the door, but it's locked. She tries feverishly to open it.

"Open the door right now."

"Calm down. I'm sure after I explain everything you still will not fully understand. But you're going to have to trust me. Now the woman that you were helping, she was pregnant."

"Where is she? Where's the baby?"

"I can assure you that she and her child are just fine."

The stranger simply extends his hand toward a chair in the side of the room, and manages to drag it across the room without even touching it, behind Latrice.

Latrice sits down. "Who are you?"

"Calm down. Please allow me to explain."

Latrice tries to run by him and makes a run for the door.

The room shifts its position so that the tall overpowering man prevents Latrice from getting there.

"Now Latrice, my name is Bryus. As you experienced, Kaylandria was pregnant."

"What happened to her?"

"Where she is, where she was, and where she will be cannot be fully explained, not to mention understood in one setting."

"Where is the child?"

"The child has life."

"Was it a boy or girl?"

Bryus walks around the lavender bedroom. The sudden overcast clouds streak across the skies and easily impede the pure sunlight that once was coming through the bedroom window. "That is a good question. You know, I have never been asked that question before. I will say this. Some believe that Kaylandria earned the right to conceive and bring forth life in a way that few women will ever get to experience."

"Who sent you?"

"That is a question that cannot be answered at this moment. However, it is important that you trust me."

"Trust you. I don't even know you."

"I'm sorry but do you always come into strange homes to help peculiar women who are expecting?"

Latrice quickly makes her way out of the room and thinks she is going into the hallway but she only walks back into the same room where Bryus is standing.

She looks back, and there's the same room once again... and again... and again... until she gives up.

Bryus says, "I mean you no harm. Please have a seat."

Latrice slowly comes back in. Bryus pulls a seat out from the corner. "Please... sit." And so she does.

Bryus sits on the corner of the bed.

"I know that you might be starting to ask yourself tons of questions. I also know that you have recently experienced a loss... or two."

Latrice says nothing.

"All right. It is important that you listen to what I say to you for the next few minutes. At the end of what I say, you will either elect to move forward or not. Either way will not offend me or the one who sent me. But be simply wants you to have a choice. Am I understood?"

Latrice continues to listen, slightly nodding her head.

"Good. Now I am not going to give you all the details but she's been with us from the very beginning of this life."

"Where was she before?"

"I do not know. But for four and a half billion revolutions around our sun, Kaylandria has withstood a true test of time and has seen much."

"I want you to let me go right now."

"When I finish talking I will. And now all that Kaylandria has absorbed was just released. That is what you just experienced, the release of a new universe. Kaylandria will be appointed over... I shouldn't say that. She will raise and be the guardian-caretaker over that which she has birthed. The one who sent me has sought a replacement and He believes that He might have found her."

Latrice says, "Who is he?"

"He is the Creator."

"So let me get this right. You were sent here to get me?"

"The Creator..."

"The Creator sent you here to get me."

"That is correct."

Latrice really doesn't know what to say to this. And she feels a little leery of this strange tall pale man.

Bryus continues, "Now let me add to that. Not that you have done any miraculous deed to deserve this measure of grace and favor, but it is by His sovereign rule that you have been chosen."

What Bryus was adding was that birth was only one of the blessings that the Creator had in store for Kaylandria.

Latrice is not trusting Bryus nonetheless, but she's feeling guilty over not being open-minded again, "And what have I been chosen for?"

"To receive an opportunity."

"I am declining your offer. Please allow me to leave."

And just like that, Bryus stands and moves to the side. Latrice does not know what to make of this.

"You may leave. But before you go, I ask that you give me one year."

There's a little hesitation.

"I am giving you seven sunsets to change your mind."

Latrice leaves the room, goes down the steps, through the front door, and down a few more front yard steps until she gets to the street. And then she turns around and looks at the mysterious home. Bryus stands in the window of Kaylandria's room.

Ch 18

At the same time over in Hampton, Rick was dealing with some serious sleep deprivation. The engineered nutrient had taken root. So he slept for unaccounted-for-hours at a time. And in between those times of work and rest, he would relax his mind by doing the simplest of things, like admiring the graphic design layout of junk mail, or searching the house for dust bunnies that he might have been ignoring.

But there's only but so much quietness that he could take. So around 2pm, Rick would make himself walk to the mailbox just for the fresh air. However, on this particular day, Rick walked outside and something was different. The colors of the trees, grass, sky, cars, telephone poles, even the street pavement was more rich and vibrant. He could even see a little further away. Rick's sense of smell was heightened. He could smell the fresh cut grass from down the street, the urine from the Doberman being walked, as well as the rain that was forecast to come later on that evening.

Rick goes into the student center on campus, walking by some of the female professors and students who smile at him. They've seen Rick Foster before, but there is a new energy that they detect. He's filling out his army green V-neck short sleeve a little differently. His chest, arms, and shoulders are moving another kind of way all together. And Rick is not even aware of it. He's walking around other people who just simply stare at him. There's nothing wrong externally with him. He's just exuding something that is resonating with the students.

Rick then checks the mail box inside the student center and pulls out his quarterly subscription to Beyond Reach, a publication dedicated solely to astronomy. Featured, was a most interesting article on a tribe of people in Western Africa called the Dogon. The article credits them with being experts on stars, both charted and uncharted.

Rick walks back out into the daylight and goes back to his lab. As he makes his way back to the lab, Rick begins to get dizzy. The nutrient had obviously begun to take effect.

CH 19

Apparently, a brain cell, of all cells in the body, was stimulated by the nutrient. Then Rick struggles to make his way over to his lab table to take note of his pulse. But he falls down to the floor.

This new altered cell within Rick's body then stimulates the strange rock which is still half way around the world in Nigeria. And on its own accord, it elevates itself from the band of mercenary thieves into the air.

At an incredible speed, the unique rock finds itself leaving central Africa, to the coast, all the way over across the Atlantic Ocean to Hampton, Virginia. And in just three minutes total, birth shall be given, to one who has never existed in all of eternity before this moment, had it not been for Rick's destined curiosity. But Rick was still pained while he lay still on the hard cold dusty floor. Struggling to stay alive, he thinks to himself, "So why is it happening to me now?"

The process of bringing this spiritual artifact from across the world has Rick on his knees, gasping for any air that he can get into his lungs. For the journey was fueled by the energy of his very own spirit.

And then a newborn presents himself in front of Rick in the form of a tall mature man, with intense eyes filled with understanding and a full working knowledge of who he was and what needed to be accomplished.

He says, "I am Arah, sent to you by the Creator. It was your believe in Him that has indeed produced this moment. You were not chosen, but rather you chose yourself. I am here merely to provide you one option. You now have within yourself unusual life that was not originally given to you. And so since it was not given to you by divine authority, but by your own hand, you are now the target of an enemy. This enemy is nowhere that you are able to locate, now. But soon life on your precious Earth will find its way into an imbalance. You, Rickland Foster, have now placed your planet and perhaps your galaxy in grave danger. The option that was given to you to work here on answers leading to the betterment of your Earth's atmosphere was brought to you by this very same enemy. His name is Onjito, an alien being of diabolical madness whose only mission is universal domination. And this means that your Earth and everything connected to it that you have come to love will fall in certain peril as well.

Rick is obviously confused and goes into immediate defense mode, "I don't know what you are talking about."

Arah responds, "Ah, I understand. You need proof. Well allow me to illustrate." Arah brings Rick in front of a mirror in the lab and he stands behind him. And in that same instant, Rick's torso begins to reveal a pure and beautiful light as gorgeous as the sun itself.

Arah is able to penetrate layers of Rick's tissue and brings forth the human cell that Rick was miraculously able to alter. He says to Rick, "What you have done has never been done by anyone on Earth."

Rick stands in complete awe. What he sees in the mirror cannot be seen by him with his naked eye when he looks down at his chest. Everything is intact. He looks at Arah in disbelief.

Arah walks around Rick's lab, slowly pacing and says, "That which was already inside of you, you have taken it upon yourself to ignite. And now you must be responsible for this action."

Rick responds, "What does that mean, responsible?"

Arah's purpose is to make Rick understand completely. He says, "The powerful cell in which you have altered now carries a unique signature of another universe of another time. You were divinely inspired to birth matter that was destined to come forth. Unfortunately, you will soon lose memory of this discovery."

Rick gets upset, "What do you mean?"

Arah responds, "However, what you could gain is a knowledge that will far surpass anything ever imagined in your wildest untamed thoughts."

Rick asks, "How?"

Arah responds, "I am afraid that I am not equipped to tell you."

Rick says, "Well then I am afraid that it is impossible for me to entertain what you are saying. Plus, I need to hang onto my memories. So, I'm really not buying what you're saying."

Arah says, "What I am equipped to tell you is that if you do not cooperate with me, then the one cell will begin to decay. Then your tissues will decay, and then next your organs, your systems, and then…"

Rick says, "Okay I get it, my body."

Arah responds, "You do not get it. What you have to understand is the one cell wants to go where it belongs. And I am here to offer you a choice."

Rick says, "Do you know how crazy you sound? You want me to go somewhere I've never been. And you cannot give me any answers." Rick is really thinking about Latrice.

Arah says, "All of the answers that you need, you already have. You created them."

Rick and Arah's voices have been heard. And their presence has been detected by others who are very near.

With one eye brow up, Rick is cautiously curious with this total stranger, whose eyes say, "Trust me."

He says to Rick, "I hope that you choose to go. That which you have inside of you, is you. And it cries out to where it belongs. I pray that you do not stand in its way."

The black metal door knob to the lab begins to twist open. Arah's right ear twitches, and he puts an arm in front of Rick. Arah turns to the door, and in comes RJ-5.

Rick sees him and says, "Senator Jacobs, what an unexpected surprise."

RJ-5 responds, "Oh but I am equally as surprised. I see you decided not to utilize the lab over at Langley."

"Everything I need is right here Senator."

Arah and RJ-5's eyes lock.

Then RJ-5 flips the switch on his tone all together and becomes slightly enraged. "I thought I asked you not to work here. You may have jeopardized this operation all together."

Rick responds, "You haven't to worry..."

RJ-5 cuts over him. "Where are your results? I have gone to great lengths to provide you with an excellent space in which to work, and you just decided on your own that you would do something completely different. How unprofessional."

RJ-5 pokes around the lab, looking at both sides of Rick's roll away chalk board, and realizes exactly what has happened. "Interesting. Would you come over and explain these equations to me?"

Arah sees right through it, "Go nowhere." The intensity in his voice just matched the one of Arah's face.

RJ-5 says to Rick, "Rick, listen to me. You are in grave danger."

Arah says nothing, and moves Rick behind him. He says to RJ-5, "I know who sent you."

RJ-5 says, "Who, the taxpayers? Rick who is this clown?"

Arah's body takes over the lab space by stretching his hands to the east and west. There's a bracelet on Arah's left wrist that catches the attention of Onjito, who continues to observe this confrontation from the privacy of his wasteland of a throne from afar. Onjito rises from his chair. "Ah, there. There!"

As Arah fixes his mouth to say that which he needs to say, the atmosphere inside the lab changes violently as if they were in the midst of a dark wind storm. He then says, "Bracelet of Urangule', grant me the favor of the Yeswe'."

Molecules of the air come to Arah's aid, bringing forth a wall, a dense blockade.

And right before Rick's very eyes, a semi-invisible wall materializes, made up of the available particles in the air, all strengthened together to form a bond. The strange wall prevents RJ-5 and his alleged Secret Service from advancing toward Rick. They try several times to force their way through the wall, but every attempt is met with failure.

In the very next continuum, Onjito gets up and pounds his mighty fist on his vessel's console and says, "But how? Five, call them back."

And in that same instant, RJ-5 and the two Secret Service detail dematerialize.

Once Arah is sure that he is gone, he calmly says, "Release." And the particles of the wall disperse, allowing the air and tiny dust particles to be as they once were.

Arah turns around to Rick. And Rick stands there in utter shock.

Arah takes the strange dark brown leathery bracelet off of him and puts it in Rick's hand. He stands in front of Rick and removes the hood of his black head garment.

He says to Rick, "If you choose to continue this journey, only then will the true secret of this bracelet be revealed.

"But a journey to where?

"Trust your instinct Rick Foster."

That made no sense at all to Rick. "What else can you tell me?"

Arah grabs Rick's hand.

Rick's eyes are blinded with the light of a vision, forcing him to quickly shut his tender eyelids. For this Light, his eyes have never seen. His mouth stays ajar, taking deep breaths to inhale to desperately and quickly understand.

He sees something so incredible, a never before spoken of world of guarded yester.

Then a Mighty voice of Valor and Strength speaks to Rick, but only in thought. "Follow me Gakuru."

"The Creator." Rick thinks. Intuitively, he knows the Voice, although he has never heard it so clear before. It is as if there was a new piece of Rick's inner ear that has been there all the while, but never before used until this instant.

Intangible, hidden, but present, the Creator reveals to Rickland that a beast lord by the name of Onjito was responsible for Latrice having her miscarriage.

Rick thinks, "What? How is this even possible?" But he knows in his spirit that what he hears is the Truth, and he has no choice but to accept it as such.

And then Rick's slumbered spirit utters a question directly to the Creator. "What wickedness was performed that caused an innocent life to be taken?"

Rick sees an image of someone so horrible, so extensively evil and then he feels the very essence of Onjito's horror which took the life of his child. And in anguish, Rick asks, "He killed my baby? Why?"

And the Creator carefully whispers the answer to into Rick's spirit.

Rick then asks, "How?"

And the Creator responds once more in an even softer whisper.

Whatever the Creator has said, it was enough to make Rick think of the space between him and Latrice. He thinks, "I wonder if there was more that I could have done."

The Creator says, "This is all that I am showing you. Your Earth, as you know it, is in danger. All things will move according to My will."

And when Rick opens his eyes, he releases a slow yell, a crescendo. "What's wrong with me? I can't see!"

Rick sees nothing. He twists the base of his palms around and presses hard into his eyes, trying to rub his precious sight back into existence. But nothing happens. With his throat tightening and breathing increasing from his frustration, Rick extends his hands, trying to feel his way to Arah, or anyone who can open his eyes, "Arah. Help me. What did you do?"

A painful minute goes by and Rick has found his way over to the corner of one of the high lab tables. And Arah comes over to Rick and touches him on the back of his head, "Trust in the Creator. You will see. And when you do, everything will come into plain sight. Now tell me, did you see anything other than what the Creator spoke of?"

Rick hesitates as he struggles to say, "I saw... I saw... it was so miraculous. I have to say that I sincerely delighted in looking out over an absolutely amazing land, on a ledge, on the highest plateau that I ever knew existed. It felt so high up, like I had stepped into another layer of the atmosphere. But even more striking than that were the people that I then encountered. I was in a great city with marvelous architecture. I placed my hands on the shoulder of so many people who needed comforting, and then they gave each other the precious work of their own hands. And once they were satisfied, they gave a portion to me. I don't understand, but all of it was so beautiful, so gentle. I've never seen a people like this, anywhere on Earth."

Arah says, "You will. Those people are your people."

"What?"

"The Creator has heard your noble cry. And he has chosen you to live amongst this first civilization of Earth inhabitants.

And then the voice of the Creator spoke once more in Rick's mind, enabling him to see that first civilization even more clear. "And I will make you Gakuru, king of Earth."

Arah says, "My purpose has now been completed. Thank you for taking such a risk and a leap of faith. For had you not listened to your heart, I would have never had this opportunity to exist. Thank you. Thank you."

Rick nervously says, "Wait! Don't leave."

Arah comes over and takes Rick's hands and bows to him. He then places his finger tips on Rick's eyelids, caressing them once.

And by the time Rick's sight was returning to him, Arah was in the act of peacefully disappearing. The air that was around him celebrates by illuminating any remaining dust particles.

Rick could only stand there, mouth open, blinking irregularly, shaking his head, with nothing but a strange leather band on his left forearm.

"How does this work? Will I need to utter some word, Bracelet of the Urangule'?"

Arah responds, "The Bracelet will tell you what to utter. Be careful. There are those in this universe who would do anything to have what you have. I trust that you use your best judgment, the kindness of your heart, and every one of your senses to make the wisest choices."

Rick really doesn't know what to say. He is just as confused as anyone would be. It's all so much to absorb. His theory and experiment produced a moment with the Creator Himself. How amazing. "My goodness."

Arah senses that Rick is overwhelmed with all that is going through his head. "Don't go into shock Rick. Allow yourself to give in to the unknown."

Rick laughs and exhales, "You know that I say that to my students."

"I know."

Arah and Rick respond simultaneously, "Why should a lack of information prevent one from having an open mind?"

Arah says, "The Creator has given me the choice of allowing you to travel by yourself or accompany you..."

Relieved, Rick says, "Oh yes. Would you...?"

Arah holds his hand up, "You must know something. You will lose memory of who you are here in this continuum, so that they may receive the full knowledge of who you will become, who you were actually born to be."

Arah spoke of the truth for Rick along another time continuum.

"Am I not just going back in time?"

"You are, however you must travel directly through the Perimeter in order to travel back that far. A human's memory has to be erased, but in this case it will be replaced."

Rick replies, "I want to see this person who is responsible for the death of my daughter, but if the Creator is allowing everything to happen, then why can't He just simply put a stop to it? Or why couldn't he have just prevented any of this from happening? Why?"

Rick gets worked up all over again, and he begins to clinch his fist together. And when he does, that activates the bracelet. Rick's controlled emotion of feeling afraid and violated reverbs an energy sphere around the room, pushing fixed lab tabled and all to the edges of the classroom. But it doesn't move Arah, as he shifts his molecular structure and avoids the energy all together.

"You must control your feelings. The Bracelet is powerful and responds to your feelings in order to protect you."

Rick just shakes his head in disbelief.

Arah says, "The bracelet was never meant to be used here. I brought it here..."

Rick interjects, "Ah I see, to lure me. Well what's waiting for me when I get there?"

"I have no answer for that."

Rick says nothing.

"You will not have any memory of this Earth in this time, along this continuum."

Arah sees the despair on his face, connected to the one he loves the most. "You may choose to remain is you wish."

Rick continues to say nothing, but displays so much confusion in his soulful eyes.

Arah says, "Stay or embark, the result will be the same. Fear can keep you from where we belong. At some point, we all have to let go… and trust."

Rick responds, "I get it."

"If you are worried about your memories of this time, think of it this way. You will understand what you love and Latrice and what separated the two of you in this time at the right time, in another time."

Rick offers a little more of an agreeable facial expression.

"Sometimes it's necessary to have a clear mind to find truth."

And then Rick says, "You know, I think that this is just way too much for me to deal with. I'm going to have to say that my answer is no. I can't. I'm just going to have to let things be as they should. It's not my place to tamper with life and time so casually."

Arah responds, "Too late."

CH 20

Meanwhile in the desert, Asani is standing on the front porch and gazes out onto his horizon. The wind is moving from left to right, with a mixture of warm and cool air. He goes down one of the two porch steps, and lurking from behind an agitated voice speaks. "I'm gonna tell you one time. That's it. You see those mountains over there? Do not go over there?" Asani turns around to acknowledge Bowers' voice, but there's something glowing, pulsating, calling out to Asani. Something is resonating with his spirit.

His curiosity begins to swell. He takes another step off the porch. Then Bowers comes from behind and lifts him from the ground by his neck and throws him fifteen feet to the left, over the side of the porch. "I am going to say this one more… one more time. Do not get any strange ideas."

Asani lands on his shoulder and dislocates it. And Bowers looks at him, "What? Do you have something to say? A rebuttal perhaps? I will whip your ass into another existence. As a matter of fact, why don't I do this?" And Asani gets up, favoring his left shoulder.

Bowers then rushes over. Asani backs up. Bowers stops, "I mean if you don't mind, please do not go in that direction." Bowers extends a hand for him to get up. Asani is hesitant. But Bowers flashes his disarming smile... making it okay for Asani to accept his hand.

And so he does. "You fool!" Bowers then kicks him in his thigh several times. "Don't say nothin' to me."

Asani can't believe it. He can't even remember the last word that he's uttered. "Where are my thoughts? I have no memory."

And then suddenly, Bowers stops. And he backs up a few steps. What's going through his head? He steps toward Asani and Asani instinctively backs up.

And with a burst of remorse, Bowers comes over. "Come here man. You know I didn't mean that." Bowers takes him by the hand and stands up straight.

And then Bowers gently applies the right amount of pressure to put his shoulder back in its proper place. "Oh yeah, you don't know how to speak. I'm Bowers. Can you say that? Bow-ers."

Asani ain't trying to hear him. He's too caught up with trying to stretch his arm out to make sure that it can rotate back and forth. But he doesn't take his eyes off Bow-ers because of his sporadic violent behavior.

Asani asks himself how is Bowers making him feel. "I do not like him, nor any of what I've awakened to."

They stop walking and they face one another. And then his grip on Asani's hand gets tighter. "All we have is each other." Bowers takes him by the hand and slings him, making Asani's arms come even more out of his socket. Yearning to still understand who he is and what is currently happening to him, Asani releases a sound for help.

Bowers understands. "I am your help."

Bowers is sitting trying to find relief for a throbbing headache. He then comes over to Asani. "How are you?"

He kneels down, exposing his teeth, and he simply starts laughing all up in Asani's face. "Now get in that house and fix me something to eat! And I do not want any dirt either."

Asani eventually drags himself through the dry rocky gravel and back into the strange house. Every room is unique, but connected. But it's hard to see as there is hardly any light throughout the house. There might be just enough light on a wall to see what's going on in each room. Even in his current pain, Asani is curious as to how the house came into existence.

On his way back to his room, he notices an open space where a very dated early 80's Apple computer monitor is. Flashing and flickering on the screen are pages to various obscure images: a bare chest Obama shackled on a slave ship arriving in Jamestown, Martin Luther King on television spraying high pressure water onto discriminated whites, Oprah Winfrey cheerfully whipping Harriett Tubman back up the steps into her master's front door, Adolph Hitler preaching and healing the masses of Jews in Jerusalem, Malcolm X on a flash flooded red carpet with Marilyn Monroe at the Academy Awards, Jesus Christ praying to Allah.

And while Asani has no clue as to what he's looking at, something about these images connect with him.

Asani is by himself. He lives alone but with the presence of another being. It breathes and has its own needs. But the two are on separate pages. Bowers has the upper hand because he knows how every single thing works in this strange house. Asani is still trying to make sense of his being, but from out of his thoughts, as discombobulated as they are, come a declaration, "I have something to say."

So Asani finds Bowers on the side of the house where he is comparing the sizes of bolts. Bowers then sparks up his blowtorch and cuts the thick metal bolts to specific sizes.

He's on the ground and says to Asani, "I'm gonna put you to work. Come here and learn something."

Bowers takes Asani under the house in the crawl space. The wiring coming up from the ground into the house is insanely complex. Thin wires grouped into clusters go from the ground to pretty much each room of the house.

There's a door off the living room that Bowers opens. He steps to the side so that Asani can see. "Dark ain't it? Now get your ass down there."

Asani takes a step down, and looks back at Bowers. "Go! Stop looking at me."

Asani continues and Bowers slams the door shut. Asani bangs on the door, "Stop. Let me out."

And Bowers mocks him, "Stop, let me out!" And he laughs at him. "That's what you get. Since you like going into dark spaces. Now I told you not to do something and you did it anyway."

Asani responds, "Yeah but come on." And then there's silence. Asani shakes his head. No one is on his side.

So Asani gives in and goes down the steps. Bowers is listening just on the other side of the door.

"Good." Bowers cuts on a light. "That should help you out. Now go down the steps." And he does. Asani goes down and discovers an entire basement level of networked wires. There are about a dozen black metal floor-to-ceiling shelves which house complicated but organized network wiring. And then Asani comes before a glass wall.

Through an intercom located on a nearby column, Bowers speaks. "Now go in."

Asani tries to push his way in but he cannot. "I can't." He looks back upstairs.

And Bowers responds, "Shut up, n' try it again!"

Asani steps forward and examines the intricate door, something that resembles a foreign writing, but Asani doesn't know the difference because everything is still very new. One eye brow up, Asani looks at it with a degree of familiarity, but it's still strange. He steps toward the door, and all of sudden, he's completely surrounded by a circular wall that has the same writing but more expanded.

The walls then begin to move in the same circular fashion. It starts out slow. Asani turns around,

"What's going on?" No answer from above. And the walls are spinning, and beginning to generate an energetic breeze. The wall begins to generate a story before his very eyes.

On the wall appears a man and his family, and they huddle together and disappear, confusing Asani that much more.

And he hears a voice, "What are you doing!" Bowers is screaming from the top of the steps. The walls come to a screeching stop. "Well obviously you did something wrong."

And Asani yells, "What am I supposed to be doing?"

There's a second of silence. Bowers is upstairs in the kitchen sitting in an old flower plastic cushioned chair eating and savoring some extremely hot bread pudding. "Figure it out."

Asani walks around the circle of walls, looking, touching, feeling, and trying to understand. Again there are five panels, all tall, stand alone, and made of some sort of stone with the smoothest of dark surfaces.

The dimensions are seven feet by three feet by four inches.

Asani walks over to one panel where he sees engraved a man standing in front of a towering gigantic muscular being. The man appears to be in no danger.

The next panel that Asani notices is one of instruction, *"from a man... a man who showed me... how to fight."* And then he remembers, *"I beat him already."* One single choreographed fighting move comes back to Asani's memory, a piece of his reality is revealed.

The third panel is one of the same man but with no eyes.

The fourth panel shows the same man looking on as his father comes into contact with a beautiful woman from a heaven.

The fifth panel is blank, and is as smooth as the skin on the backside of a baby. But Asani gets the impression that the dark greyish green surface doesn't represent emptiness.

He angrily makes his way back upstairs, finds Bowers outside in the dusty front yard, and commences to whippin' his ass. It starts off as a slow ass beating because he's not really sure, but it's all about him trying to get a grasp on his vague past. And he ends up really whipping Bowers good.

"Stop. Stop it."

They find their way back inside the house and they sit at the kitchen table. And Asani asks, "What's wrong with you?"

Bowers is placing a cold white facecloth on his fat swollen bottom lip. "Well nothing now. I too was asleep in my stasis chamber just like you, only to be awakened by the Spirit Rhaija. She came to me in a dream. And I remember being forced to watch horrific acts of disgrace. It was like... no, she did... she turned me on myself. There were things that I've never seen before, places that I've never been, yet they were all familiar."

And in that moment, Asani knew that Bowers was describing similar feelings that he was having.

Bowers pleads, "Asani, you're actually helping me to get rid of it."

"What did you just call me?"

"Asani, that is your name."

Asani goes back downstairs to face the walls again. The missing elements of the last panel materialize. Asani sees a remnant of people who stay behind on some world, seeing and hope for a safe return.

Still tending to his swollen lip, Bowers walks up behind Asani. "You see, before you were awakened, this being whom is referring to himself as Five put some sort of spell on me to keep kicking your ass, you see. And the best way for him to do that was to use what has already been done to our people for ages, since The First Departure."

Asani continues to study the pictures on the strange underground walls while he absorbs everything that Bowers is saying. "I want to know more, but I don't know if I can trust you. Who are you?"

Bowers responds, "That is a fair question. As you begin to understand who you are, you will remember me."

Asani approaches Bowers, "Where are we?"

"Let's just say that we are not where we should be."

Asani says, "How do you know all of this?

"I know what I know because of where I have been and where I know we will be once again."

Bowers goes to the only basement window and looks eye level at the dark gravel as it kisses the grey overcast sky. "Everything will be revealed as it should, when it should."

Asani walks away back up the steps, leaving Bowers standing in the basement.

And who can blame Asani? He has so many questions that need answers.

Bowers yells, "Asani! I'm sorry. But time is running out."

Cʜ 21

Asani continues to stand at the top of the steps. And in a quiet agitated voice, he hears Bowers, "Now get your ass over here right... I'm playing. Come here for a second."

Asani slowly comes over to Bowers, who is desperately trying to regain control of his mind. But Five has certainly done a job on him.

Bowers asks, "Who are you?"

And Asani looks away, "I don't know."

Asani and Bowers look in to each other's eyes without blinking.

And then the five tall stone tablets in the basement begin to dissolve down into the floor. Asani takes notice and Bowers says, "Come on. Follow me."

Bowers leads Asani back upstairs in a hurry. But Bowers leaps all sixteen noisy steps at once, leaving Asani to wonder, "How did he just do that?"

And then 5 rods begin to slowly emerge from the ground around the perimeter of the house.

Bowers responds, "See these rods? There are five rods buried around the house. Wait. Do we need to take a moment to remind you how to count? What we, excuse me, what you are going to do is pull each one of these rods up out of the ground. Then you are going to walk each one, one at a time to someone who will then take them from you."

Asani takes one look at the first rod. "Why am I taking these rods away from the house?" And Bowers, after a second of deliberation, says, "Don't ask me any questions. Walk around the house and collect the rods like I just said."

Bowers starts to twitch, his neck, his shoulders, like something just dug his hand into his back.

He turns to Asani. "Listen, I know I told you to go... you know... over there. But, once you find Five, you will introduce yourself to him and leave the rods with him."

Bowers stops and he shakes something off of him. "Look, take this."

He was about to send Asani off in the right direction, until he starts trippin' out. Bowers closes eyes and starts bobbing his head and finds a little space to do a little dance. And then he says to Asani, "You know what, that's okay, start him out with just this one. But say to him. 'I am here to offer this as a gift.'"

And Asani asks, "Who is Five?"

Bowers replies, "You will go to Five and say exactly what I have just said to you. Am I understood?"

Asani nods his head, but really isn't sure what the hell is going on.

And then Bowers' head twitches left. "On second thought, wait."

And Bowers walks around to another side of the house, leaving Asani confused. "First he says don't go, then go, then don't go."

Asani weighs everything that was just said by Bowers and he decides to go in the direction of Five. He doesn't know why. But everything is so new. Why let fear stand in the way? But first Asani goes into the house when he realizes that his mouth is dry again.

He goes to the room where his stasis chamber is and looks at the tubes. He lifts the hose up for it appears to be water leaking out.

There's plenty of light outside and Asani has an abundance of curiosity, despite his senseless injuries.

CH 22

With this first rod, Asani walks across the desert, towards an energy that continues to intrigue him. And he thinks to himself, "How did I get here?"

Hours later, Asani walking leads him to a dark passage through a high range of mountains, and then into a valley.

Eyes are on Asani, but none that can be detected. However they speak, "Come to me." Asani looks down to his left and right.

The path through the mountain range ends in the center of a valley, where Asani finds himself standing in a circular space, approximately 40 yards in diameter. To his left, Asani looks around and notices a path that leads into an obscure cave.

With the first rod in hand, Asani walks into the cave and walks about 100 feet until he hits a dead end.

"Who are you?" Asani just stands there with his golden rod.

Five takes a good look at Asani. "So is there something that you have for me? Tell me you didn't walk all this way just to give me one rod."

Something strange happens to the wall at the end of the dark corridor. There's an archway about seven feet high and it creates an opening in the wall. Half of it disappears. And Asani sees sights of chaos among others who look like him going on about in the background.

And Five, smirks. "You have questions do you not?"

Asani is enticed a little by what he sees. And then the background of people is wiped away and replaced with the house from where he just arose. Bowers is angrily walking the property. "Where are you?"

Asani gives Five the shiny rod.

Five says to Asani, "Bring me another rod and I will tell you more." Asani turns around and asks him the same.

And Five answers, "Soon."

CH 23

"**W**here do you live?" Five asks.

Asani responds, "Live?"

Five examines the rod. "Yes, where do you live? Do you live alone? What's the matter with you? Don't you know how to talk?"

Asani interjects, "I live with Bowers. When I opened my eyes, there he was. He did not want me to leave and I don't know why. I mean first he said go, then he... I don't know."

Five is trying to wrap his mind around Asani's thoughts. "Interesting. Are there any more of these rods? I really like them."

Five takes the rod back through the strange portal with him. And Asani tries to follow him but a strange invisible force deliberately pulls him back. Five turns around with a look of concern.

"Hmm…" Five then extends the rod towards Asani and the force pulling him away from the strange opening loses some of its power, but only for a brief moment. The pull re-engages itself, forcing Asani to leave the cave all together.

Five yells, "Sorry about that. Come on back when you get a chance!" The strange pull tosses Asani outside the cave, onto his backside. He gets up and gets pulled back down. He gets up again and gets pulled right back down on his back. Asani gets up a third time and gets pulled back down once more.

He sighs and while on his back he stares into the sky. He turns his head toward the entrance to the cave. And the entrance is no more.

Still on his back, Asani's eyes expand and embraced the width of the reddish sky. He then saw a glimpse of two men. One was Bowers. And the other was himself.

This image of Asani says, "I had traveled a long journey." And what he saw, he saw no more. Asani successfully gets up. But he's puzzled. With his intense brow of discrepancy, Asani's strong dark eyes shift from left to right. He's accepted the challenge of surviving in a foreign land while trying to discover who he is.

Asani goes back to touch the entrance to the cave but nothing happens to its hard coal-like surface.

Ch 24

In the meantime, Latrice is sitting at her dining room table all alone. She can feel the blood actually flowing through her veins. All you can hear is the sound of her fork cutting down into a delicious piece of spinach lasagna. Savoring that bite of food meant so much to her. She experiences happiness because she can please herself in her ability to cook. Thank God for her happiness' sake.

Everything is so silent. Something is not right. There should be, could be something else happening, literally.

Latrice looks around at what she's amassed in her home. Her favorite sweet red tulips that keep her company, her grandmother's antique phone in the circular foyer with a warm off-white crown molding, the square gold area rug that sits on her immaculate honey hard wood floors, and the mysterious painting of a yellow background that steps the eye into white nothingness. Since Rick had pretty much cleaned her out, Latrice has used this as a perfect opportunity to pull items from her storage unit that represented love and healing.

This is the world that she has had to rebuild for herself. Latrice's flawless pretty feet carry her over their solid hard wood floors, never hearing a creek, and in thought as she realizes now that creating happiness for herself needs to step up to a new level.

As she sits to the silence of the full presence of her perfect stillness, Latrice tries to skip through the years of all of her many work accomplishments, and then back to where she is in this silent home, and then to her past which offered much hope of love with Rick, and then back to where she is. And then she tries to take a step forward into her future, but the strength of her silence confines her to the now. Sadness desires to overtake her.

Just yesterday, Latrice was sitting in a busy Starbucks reading in her favorite orange and grey sweats. A tall lean gentleman comes over to her table where there's an empty seat. "Excuse me, I just feel like being nice. Could I please offer you a beverage?"

And Latrice freezes. "Well I just had a cup of coffee before you sat down."

That was a lie.

But there are many random men that find it easy to admire Latrice as she goes here and there. No string of words seems to be nice enough to be initiated on a man's part for Latrice to be receptive. It's as if she's protecting something. What she really yearns for is a real connection. "Maybe I'm asking for too much."

Cн 25

Later on that same evening, Latrice goes to sit in her private room of intimate thought. If only she had someone to enjoy her moment with.

She gives herself permission to go onto www.meetmyking.net and she begins to comb through the online dating profiles. She thinks, "I can't believe it's come to this." What are her filters? What makes her click on one picture vs. another?

She frowns her face as she looks at her available choices, "His nose is funny", "His eyes bulge out too much.", "He has no shirt on.", "What's his problem?" Latrice's inner thoughts are just running amuck over these scoundrels on her computer screen.

She tries adjusting the age range and the same thing happens. "Cute but ridiculous."

And then Latrice comes across one profile picture of a strange man lying in the sand. Her mouth literally drops. "Why in the world is this guy lying in the middle of the sand? Look at his fine ass. Mm."

Yeah, look at him indeed Latrice. His beautiful muscular neck, his yummy full lips that expose just a little of his pure white teeth. Everything on him is just perfect.

"Maybe he's a model or something."

His name is Asani. And he is doing a great job of selling the look that he seeks the true meaning of life. The intensity of his face just pulls Latrice right out of her seat, so much so that she moves the cursor on her computer screen to Send a Message. But she holds off.

She says aloud, "He has nothing written on his profile! How in the world am I supposed to know who this person is? He could be anyone."

What Latrice was really thinking was, "Oh, you can get it."

And he could. Latrice closes her eyes, sucking on her savory bottom lip, imagining that her perfect tits are being caressed by this man's seemingly soft strong hands.

She drums her perfect natural nails on the glass cover on her desk and starts to shut her computer down. But before she does, Latrice puts a little smiley face in the subject line of a blank note and hits *Send*.

Ch 26

Elsewhere, Asani is walking back from the valley to the strange house from whence he was awakened. But to his surprise, the house is gone. "Where did it go?"

He looks around. And Asani doubles back. "I must have walked back in the wrong direction."

Asani remembers Bowers knocking him onto the ground and feeling the soil's texture. Asani reaches down and gets a handful. "No, or did I just get lost?"

"Hey!" Asani does a 180 and there's Bowers, waiting on the porch. "I'm right here. You don't even know where you live!"

He hops off the wooden porch where there should be a rail and runs directly at Asani. Bowers cuffs Asani into a head lock. "Well?"

And Asani stands with this crazy man with a straggly stringy mustache on him, cutting off his circulation. "Get off of me."

There are a couple of things going on simultaneously. Bowers is still under Five's spell, which holds his force through the Spirit Rhaija. And Bowers is also going overboard in being playful with Asani, which he typically is. But he's way too playful which is a side effect of Five's spell.

Bowers says to Asani, "Punk ass, where is it?"

Asani breaks free and takes a step back. "Where's what?"

Bowers starts chasing him. "Do not lie to me!"

But then he just stops, like a switch was flipped for something.

"All right. I am going to give you another rod. And just like you did the last time, you are going to go back and give it to Five. And he will... he's supposed to give you something in exchange."

Though different from the spell that Five placed on Dr. Vincent, this is a powerful spell that Bowers is now under.

Asani interjects, "Well, he didn't give me anything, but…"

And he stops, and Bowers notices. "But what!" Bowers twitches like something is seriously the matter with him, swallowing bitter saliva.

"Look, take this rod, go back to Five. Now go. And get back here immediately." Bowers then steps to the side, and there standing out of the ground behind him is the second rod, same size, different in appearance. Asani walks over to the rod and examines it.

Bowers gets impatient. "Go!"

Asani walks back across the vast wasteland. He examines the second rod. It has diagonal spiral markings. It is beautiful, regal, a very charming piece.

Asani asks himself, "Why?" But everything is still so new, yet familiar. Something needs his attention, but what? Those thoughts create a nervous energy that quickened Asani's pace, and he finds himself at the cave's entrance once more. And there is Five, waiting on a smooth place while enjoying the coolness that the cave's shadow offers. But Five's large sized eyes are closed. And Asani notices that he is rocking back and forth a little chanting some sort of gibberish.

That chanting keeps him concentrated on being present in this time and in this place. If he stopped prematurely, Five would disappear. And that did not need to happen, especially now. But he does manage to finish.

"Great Erydia, you're back!"

Five looks at the rod. "May I?"

He smiles as he reaches his skinny little decrepit arm toward the rod. The question is more like a directive. Asani gives Five the second rod because those nasty nails of Five are a horrible shade of off yellow and olive green.

Asani asks, "What is Erydia?" Five continues to examine the rod, almost not believing that he has it. He sighs nothing but happiness, bringing attention to his sinister smile which pushes up Five's rather fat slimy green cheeks.

Asani says, "You promised to tell me about this King and some woman."

"Hmm? Oh! Yes. A very long time, in another time ago, in another space, there was a King who ruled over a new foreign land. He was a new ruler and quickly learned that he could not meet the needs of his kingdom by himself. While this King had a gift in wisdom, he lacked insight in spiritual matters. So one day he met a spiritual witch, a sorceress, named Kaylandria. And he appointed her as his spiritual counselor. But the King would soon grow jealous over Kaylandria's spiritual gift, and would soon thereafter send her into exile, putting her in a place where only he could access her. And that place was called Erydia, the home of Kaylandria. There she was free to see and hear all that concerned her Kingdom."

Asani responds, "So is she real? Where is Erydia?" Five ignores Asani and continues to talk.

"And since she was blessed to be in a place of connecting with the King's subjects, the King was a little intimidated by her. She was indeed the first of her kind. This zealous spiritual leader got into one too many differences of opinion with the king and she and her spiritual clan were gently escorted into exile."

And Five thinks to himself, "That's enough."

But he tells Asani, "Let's move on. There's another rod. Go back to Bowers and get me the next rod. Hurry now. There is more that I want to share."

CH 27

Now as Asani and Five wrap up their discussion, Latrice Foster just so happens to be examining Asani's picture on the dating website. She thinks, "I'm gonna find me some happiness, one way or another."

She begins to allow her mind to create a wonderful day with him. "Can you hear me Asani?"

While Asani is trekking across the dark reddish desert plain in the heat, he hears a voice. It sounds so inviting but he cannot make any sense out of it. And Asani closes his eyes.

He opens his eyes, and Asani finds himself sitting in the dark beautiful room in front of Bower's janky homemade computer, back at the very quiet ranch style home. "How did I get back here?"

One strange light from the ceiling casts itself down on Asani to allow him to see. He sits with his back facing to the opening of the large empty room. Heaven forbid that he look out into the pitch blackness of the hallway.

Cн 28

The *1984 McIntosh computer monitor* is snowy and the tiny red light at the corner of the dirty second hand crème hard drive is very strong. The piece of masking tape that holds the front cover on could use a little reinforcement. Bowers appears from the hallway as Asani presses the tape with his manly thumb.

Somehow, by Latrice using the Meet My King website, she has connected with ease to Asani, who is nothing more than a strange and good looking man to Latrice. But on her end, Latrice hears the movement as she sits with one foot cocked in the cushion of her favorite sitting chair. "Hello?"

She gets the most beautiful visual of Asani on her LCD monitor, and just as he sits down. She thinks, "Well hello Mr. Meet My King."

Asani says nothing, but rather gives Latrice a curious stare filled with strength and innocence.

Bowers slowly walks up on Asani, "Man let me tell you something…"

Latrice quickly reaches for the mouse to terminate the session, but accidently only servers the video feed. She can still hear.

Bowers comes over and twists Asani around using the green back of a 1945 retro desk chair. "Keep your chit chat to a minimum."

Asani responds, "Nothing was said."

"Good."

"Don't play yourself."

"I don't even know her."

"Keep it that way."

Latrice is nervously listening. She's careful to make sure the mute button is on.

"Do we have any family, friends… anywhere else here?"

Bowers says nothing as he looks away from Asani.

That made Latrice look around at the dark emptiness of her new home and she sighs heavily. She leans her bare shoulder up against the wall in the hallway as she listens to them.

At the same time, that strikes a certain memory with Bowers.

Bowers suddenly recalls, "Family is absolutely everything to me. When my parents were killed in the mountains, it produced a void of loneliness. And I became much more standoffish. The pain of death is something that I never wanted to experience again. What you don't know is I loved to connect with people, and treated people with kindness, never taking anyone for granted. One of the most memorable moments for me as a child was watching how my father loved my mother. They had no problems expressing their love for one another. I used to always love hearing about how they had found each other."

Bowers really hopes that Asani trusts him enough to try to understand, "They both met in the Darkness, stumbling upon one another in a quest for shelter and food." Their families were yet to become a part of the Fold. Their families hunted together and ate together, for both of their families desired to connect as well. But my parents, Mera and Remi, enjoyed playing in the unknown. Their sense of adventure is what attracted them to each other. They would spend countless hours sharing maps of places that their parents had traveled to and explored. It was so clear that they had an unquenchable thirst for the unknown, and for each other. But sometimes it's just time to sit down. Those two young people would volunteer to go to places that no one wanted to go. They knew that the places that their parents were hesitant in going, would be the places that they could go and just be themselves. Sajan was born not too long after that. And the news of the Love Explorers' child had come to the ears of the King.

Asani smiles as he's swiveling in the old worn out chair with his feet propped on the base. "So wait. Your real name is Sajan?"

"If you're going to laugh, I will stop."

Asani sits on his laugh. "Please continue."

Bowers says, "By the way, have you tried figuring out how you're able to speak so well?"

Asani responds, "What do you mean?"

Latrice had to endure listening to that. The weight of what was just said has slain her spirit, and she lays silently, eyes filled with tears, remembering what she herself had lost.

Asani asks, "Where were you born?"

Bowers takes a second to process that, "I was born in Africa on the shores of Northern Africa.

That was somewhere near what is now known as Tunisia. While Bowers originally considered that to be home, he was raised all over Pangea. His parents Mera and Remi were Kingdom workers in the area of expansion. Their jobs were to search out new places for a growing population to migrate and live. And that kept little Sajan traveling all of the time.

Bowers recalls, "There was never a moment in my childhood that I can say that I was truly settled in what I could call a home."

Cʜ 29

The next afternoon is overcast. Latrice is somehow inspired to return to the strange yet alluring Victorian style home. Her curiosity and a need to get her mind off of Rick leads her back up the strange creaking grey steps of Kaylandria's house.

She peaks through the lower glass of the door. The intensity of her breath which is fogging up the glass is an indication that she's anxious.

She knocks. But no one comes.

She gets startled. "So you decided to come back?"

Bryus is there on the porch, sitting very still in a rocking chair.

He looks at his nails and stands up. "I was really hoping that you would come to your senses."

Latrice, who stands still and looks upon Bryus in his long clergy type garment, says, "I have some questions."

Gesturing to the front door with his hand, he responds, "Good. Shall we get started?"

Bryus comes over and tries to open the door, but it won't open."

"Oh shoot. Don't tell me that I locked myself..."

He sighs. And then reaches into his pocket for the keys.

Latrice asks nothing, but she just observes. All she wants to really do is go and understand more about Kaylandria.

Bryus takes a somewhat rusty key with the edges almost worn away and tries to stick it in, but he cannot seem to twist the old brass doorknob. "I'm afraid that I might have the wrong key."

Bryus continues to search his person, Latrice comes over and looks inside once more. She puts her hand on the knob, and is able to twist the knob and open the door.

"Oh. Well how did you do that?"

"It was just open."

"Hmm. No matter."

And they both go inside.

"What a charming home!", Latrice thinks. She cannot help but to take in everything. It feels familiar to her. The beautiful warm yellow tones that caress the walls that are just so tranquil, the orchid and green pattern on the pillows with the fringes on the cream colored sofa, reminds Latrice of her late grandmother, who gave a similar warm touch to the Fosters' home when they were married.

Bryus says, "Look around. I think you're going to like this place."

Bryus' cadence and tone are accompanied by an ever so slight refined lisp.

"You talk as if I'm going to move in."

And Bryus smirks.

"The first floor is so beautiful. So what else do you know about Kaylandria?"

Bryus squints at Latrice with his narrow little soulless beady eyes. "Direct, I see. I will share with you what I know. Kaylandria ruled the Earth and now she is going to be placed over an entirely different universe."

Latrice says, "Excuse me? I came expecting the unexpected, but now I'm a little lost."

"Seems hard to believe, but that is what I am here for, to assist you in your transitionary phase."

Latrice has no idea what that even meant, but her curiosity and courage allow her to remain open minded.

Two rooms away, in their line of sight, some thing emerges from the kitchen. Latrice sees it and is not sure what to make of it. One would think that it was being blown in her direction, but she feels nothing. It sounds like a mix between cars going by and a loud refrigerator motor.

Bryus steps forward and says, "Do not move. There is an entity inside the kitchen and it is about to lash out at us."

Latrice asks, "Why?"

The entity then hurls itself at them as a dark wave of energy with the intent to harm. But it stops in midair. By that time, Latrice has taken a baby step backwards.

Bryus stands relaxed with his arms behind his back and he turns back to see a fearful Latrice, "I told you not to move."

Bryus then takes his hands and points for the strange tar-like entity to scurry off into the next room over. The walls of this room are dark mauve with baby toys arrested to the walls.

Just as Latrice rushes over to see where the strange dark entity had trounced off to, she catches it going into a strange rather fat Bugs Bunny like doll with overalls, a checkered shirt, with a little red tie, standing up in the middle of the old wooden floor.

Latrice stands at the dark doorway to the room. "You know what? I think this was a mistake."

But Bryus had come directly into her personal space and was already standing several feet over her. "You no longer have to be concerned or frightened. I can assure you that the Abiale' will no longer bother you.

Latrice says, "Aba who?"

"You are safe from Abiale', as long as you remain here with me. This sinister being Abiale' is here in the house to discard any uninvited guest, evil doers, or intruders. The exception is if they are accompanied by the owner, which in this case there is no owner. And therefore the Abiale' has to consider me as its caretaker, because I take care of this home."

Latrice makes an observation that there is a bed in the living room. "Have you been living down here on the first floor? Or has someone else been living down here?"

"Oh Latrice, that is nonsense. It a humungous house and it gets rather cold up there. The furnace is in the basement. So the heat travels here on the ground floor the fastest."

The strange bunny begins to send off a vibrating tingling sensation that grabs both of their attention. And then the four foot stuffed rabbit begins to stiffly but quickly make its way out of the room.

Bryus takes Latrice's hand and literally yanks her several feet towards a dark chestnut door with a brass knob, "So the question is what to do with this house. I want you to stay in it. Shall we go upstairs?"

And Bryus places Latrice's hand on the knob. "Open it?"

Bryus adds, "You should."

The bunny gets up to a brisk pace but the door shuts as it closes the distance.

Bryus and Latrice stand at the bottom of a dark enclosed long flight of steps. Latrice begins to breathe heavy out of her fear of tight spaces.

"Please, can we go?" And she tries to open the door to step out. But the curious look of the Abiale' filled bunny is there looking up at Latrice.

Bryus snatches the door shut. And the Abiale' kicks and releases as screeching howl.

Latrice covers her ears.

Bryus says, "Do not worry. It will not harm nor destroy any part of the house."

Latrice looks up towards the top of the steps.

Bryus says, "Follow me."

They go up the dark staircase.

Bryus says, "Kaylandria told me that she gave you a key."

"Oh yes. Here."

And then a familiar voice from a woman in a strange but elegant framed traced photo with a white background says, "Do not."

That forces Latrice to drop the key onto the step. Bryus immediately goes for it and picks it up. He turns around there, and he faces Kaylandria at the top of the step.

As he stands wide eyed, she waves her hands, sending Bryus back down the steps, out of the door and onto his back. He tumbles and lands so hard that he fractures a rib. And the Abiale' releases itself from its rodent type enclosure and overtakes Bryus, suffocating him, making him gasp for several long seconds. And the Abiale' drags the strange tall pale man into the white kitchen with the green and white checkered floor.

Latrice is scared stiff.

Kaylandria then says to Latrice in a most pleasant and calm demeanor, "Now then, shall we talk about this house?"

Several moments later, Latrice is sitting with Kaylandria at the top of the steps in a gorgeous sun drenched bay window with the finest white window treatments.

"So you really did give birth? You look so different and beautiful. Oh my goodness."

Kaylandria wants to offer a smile but really doesn't feel that it's appropriate. "All that I am, I am because of the Creator, as you will learn."

The new resonance in Kaylandria's voice is one that she herself has to get used to, or else she would shake the house and the entire eastern seaboard apart.

So Kaylandria quiets herself by closing her eyes for a second, and finds the control she needs to speak as she once did. Kaylandria takes the key from Latrice and goes to the first of several doors on the floor.

"This key unlocks the second level of this home and allows one to access mysteries of this universe. Like all homes, they have to have a date of construction. This home was initially constructed right around when the earliest settlers came to this region.

Another form of this current home was removed from Erydia long ago but shortly after the Great Departure."

Latrice replies, "Excuse me. What did you just say?"

"About what?"

"The Great Departure?"

"Yes, what about it."

Latrice did not feel comfortable sharing what Asani had shared with her. Their conversations were obscure but extremely special. So she decides to keep them tucked away. "Nothing. You just made me think about someone."

Kaylandria continues, "I knew that Gonondrius would try to come back to the Earth. But in order to do so, he would need to unlock the rooms in this house."

"Who is Gonondrius?"

"You will learn. It will not be much, but you have been afforded some time in which to learn. Some will not understand, and so you must trust me."

Latrice looks at Kaylandria.

"Now, each room contains two keys which belong to each of the Earth's original 14 territories. But here is your possible dilemma. You have to keep the doors locked. But at the same time, you face an enemy that you have no knowledge of."

Latrice fixes her mouth to speak.

Kaylandria intercepts her thought. "And before you ask, I cannot give you that knowledge, for it would deprive you of the journey that is required of you. The unlocking of each room could have devastating consequences to the entire Earth. Each unlocked room will move one continent to its original position from four and half billion years ago. But none of the continents will move until all rooms to the upstairs are unlocked. With that said, you need to unlock six of the rooms in order to know who and what you are dealing with."

And all of that just confused the hell out of Latrice. "I'm sorry. You want me to move what and stick a key into where?"

Kaylandria looks at Latrice and says nothing.

Latrice shrugs her shoulders, "Well?"

Kaylandria continues to hold her silence. She wants to say something but a greater Power is saying to her, "You're doing just fine."

Latrice then asks, "Could you at least tell me why I was chosen?"

Kaylandria feels just fine with this question. "I believe once you have a completed your journey, you will be able to answer that for yourself. My task here is now done. Where I have finished, you must now begin."

Kaylandria, who is now levitating herself inches from the floor, extends her soft but strong hand to touch her face. She hears the Creator's voice whispers, "Trust me."

Like a feather of an eagle being carried on a pallet of wind, Kaylandria allows herself to gently fall backwards down the steps.

Latrice tries to follow, but Kaylandria says as she descends, "No. You cannot."

A warm but strange yellow light from downstairs envelops Kaylandria and blinds Latrice at the same time. And then Kaylandria was nowhere to be found.

Latrice is alone once more.

So then she turns around and tries to decide which upstairs room to start with. The first door on the right seems to be singing out ever so sweetly to Latrice.

Latrice sticks her key into the door of the first room. She's quite scared. There is no one in this house. She hesitates and pulls the key out.

"Bump this."

She hits the first step to go back downstairs and the door at the bottom of the steps shuts hard and quick, leaving Latrice almost in utter darkness. The only thing to do is to go forward.

Latrice goes back and then places the key in the door. As soon as she does, she hears a vaguely familiar male's voice. "I want you to hear something."

She's intrigued. Latrice has heard the voice before. She finally unlocks the door and slowly opens it. She stands in the threshold, still dark. Very slowly, a light illuminates from the surface. She takes a step forward. She is outside, and not in the hallway. Her feet feel a little heavy, as if her physical movement was a little restricted.

The strange but familiar male voice continues, "I have always been interested in matters concerning my immediate survival. I've been known to be very practical but at the same time ambitious."

The strange voice actually belongs to Bowers, but it has yet to register with Latrice. His voice is still new to her. She sees a younger version of Bowers (Sajan) as a boy in foreign attire.

The powerful yet soft voice continues to speak, "When I was a very young adult, I got the attention of someone with an invention that allowed me to make contact with other beings and civilizations beyond our beloved Earth. But the window of communication was always very narrow and unpredictable."

Latrice stands with her eyebrows pushed in, taking everything in. "Who are you?"

Bowers continues, "One rainy afternoon, that someone ran into a group of young men all assembled by a tree, on a rainy day, by the shore, on the sand of a beach. And there stood several portals that would appear and disappear. The master scientist, Prince Antonias, was that person. He pulled me to the side that day and told me something that I've never forgotten. He told me that what I had was a gift, and that it would be needed one day for a great purpose."

While Latrice is in this space, a rather large prism appears. This Prism of Erydia reveals certain truths of the one who happens to view it.

As Latrice gazes upon its beauty, her eyes begin to bulge as she recognizes someone coming into focus, "Oh my goodness. It's the guy from Meet My King!"

She then sees Bowers coming into focus, standing in the room with Asani at the desk in front of their janky pieced together computer.

She presses onto the prism. "Asani!"

But the two men have no clue that Latrice can even see them.

She says once more while pressing her entire body onto the transparent surface, "Asani! Can you hear me? It's me!"

Meanwhile in the kitchen, the Abiale' has transformed itself into a compressed holding cube that imprisons Bryus while he holds his hands over his ears saying, "Yes, I can hear you!" And the stuffed bunny doll is there to keep him company.

Latrice continues to look and listen as Bowers continues speaking to Asani. "Prince Antonias, your father, invited me to come and study as his apprentice, and to serve the people of his kingdom with my gift of ingenuity. Little did either one of us know that those portals would get the attention of a peculiar Spirit entity."

With the wiping of his hand from left to right, Bowers conjures up an advanced holographic geographical map, "Look at this portion of time. How did this portion affect our people, your ancestors? Religion, philosophies of government and societies as well as other organized doctrines spread from what is known now as the Middle East, to Europe, and became a tool to be used to win over the hearts and minds of civilizations worldwide. The better question is where and why? Well I might suggest to you that this movement, the way that the Earth is currently, was birthed as a result of the decision of one man, King Gakuru, your grandfather, and the Earth's last Ruler."

Latrice's eyes marvel at what she sees. "What in the world?" She turns around looking for the door and can't find it. The space that she now stands in is nothing short of wondrous. Latrice stares at a man, standing roughly six foot and three inches tall, almond colored skin, a rugged man, with every muscle in his body well developed from head to toe. His eyes are filled with nothing but alertness and anticipation.

And then, all of a sudden, dear Latrice finds herself sitting in the comfort of her own home, in front of her computer and a window pops up and reads, "X748 is Now Available to Chat." Her thoughts drift a little and she finds herself going back and forth between her home and the mysterious room in Kaylandria's house. It was enough for Latrice to just burst out into screaming, "What are you doing? Make this... please make this stop, now!"

Latrice was bent over in dizziness, reminding her of Rick's driving to the hospital. And in between the transition of those rooms, Latrice is able to pick up the voice of Bowers as he continues to reveal some details to Asani, "For you see in the Beginning... after the world was created, the very first inhabitants of the Earth had dominion over the entire planet. The Earth was not how it is now."

Latrice and Asani both utter the same question in their heads, "How would you know?"

The raspy voice of Bowers responds, "Well, I should know because I was there, at the very beginning. The land masses were not as spread apart. As a matter of fact, they were not spread out at all. The territory was one united land mass. And so the land and its people, who looked like you and me, required at least one leader. Our scientists were truly remarkable. We were advanced, even relative to present day Earth standards. Mathematics, the sciences, the study of life, it all came to us rather easily. Some think that it was a gift from the Creator himself, something that would give us an advantage to understanding this unexplainable gift of life. But that conquest was not good enough. In no time at all, King Gakuru had the understanding of the Earth, and how the Earth sat upon 14 individual and separate plates. So he designated 14 rulers over his territories. Setting up these territories meant that Gakuru and his wife would be constantly going from one to the other. Understand that in the beginning, the Earth was dark and obscure. The land was vast and there was plenty of defining to be done. And so for that time, there were a people who were fit to live then, for that time specifically, the beginning. We were filled with brilliant ideas, innovations, philosophies and the means to bring just about everything to pass."

The mild flickering of Latrice's body going from one place to another reminds her of that car sick feeling on the way to the hospital. She wants to throw up but she holds it in.

And then Latrice is able to make out a concept-sketch of a familiar looking pyramid materialized before her very eyes.

Bowers continues to say to Asani, "The problem was there became a quest for even more power, more exploration, more knowledge, and more access to absolutely everything imaginable. We became possessed with our own conquest for the vastness of the unknown. Instead of cultivating what was given to us, we were enticed from our place of blessedness. Life does not have to be the search for more power. There is more to search for in life other than authority. And that includes knowledge. Had we only managed what we had, things would not have been set into motion as they are today. But we needed to have more. And so therefore, we departed, departed from our home, from our people, from our true legacy, from our beginning, from our truth, our future, and now our present. The day of our Great Departure was truly a sad day. While we were rejoicing that our curiosities were being appeased, we were enticed from what belonged to us."

And then Latrice hears Kaylandria's voice, "Close your eyes."

She's reluctant, but she has nothing to lose. So she shuts her eyes.

"Don't just hear the words, feel the words."

"What do you mean?"

"Trust your thoughts. So as you think, whatever thoughts are pure, whatever thoughts are honest, you may have, as you move between rooms, if you only believe."

And Kaylandria's voice fades away.

Latrice opens her eyes. She clears her throat a little. There's not that much saliva in her mouth. She's nervous because she's pieced together a little of what's going on.

Bowers then gets up and strolls out of the room, until the darkness of the hallway has enveloped him. Bowers' steps get more quiet as he walks down the creaky hard wood floors.

Kaylandria's voice says to Latrice, "Are you going to talk to him or not?"

It does not take a being from another universe to see that for the first time in a long while, Latrice just wants to be daring and take a chance. Somebody just needs to give her permission. So she goes and puts on something hella sexy. Just for him to see. But when she comes back and sits in her favorite chair with the dark wood back and soft olive green suede cushion, all that she can see is something kind of distorted. Well, somewhere between nothing and something. All that they can see of each other is a soft shadowy silhouette.

Kaylandria says Latrice, "Your thoughts are still not clear."

Asani says to Latrice, "How are we able to see?"

Latrice says, "Get out of my head."

Asani frowns a little, "What?"

Latrice sighs and smiles, "I'm sorry. I um.

Kaylandria's voice says, "Do not reveal to him."

Latrice responds in thought to her, "Reveal what?"

Latrice says to Asani, "It's called a webcam."

Kaylandria says to Latrice, "That's not the truth."

Asani snaps his fingers. "Yes, a web cam. I need to get one of those."

Latrice, being her cute lil' self, adds, "You probably need a better one. How come I can't see you? All I can see is a shadow. Please don't tell me that you are one of those tech-geeks who know how to manipulate your image? You and your house look dark."

Asani can't explain it. "Yeah, well I guess that's how you're coming out too. It's your fault."

Latrice says, "What?"

Asani leans back in his seat, head cocked back to the side, licking his lips and smiling, "I'm sorry. Just having a little fun."

Latrice smirks and raises an eye brow, "At my expense."

Asani says, "No. Not at all."

But from Asani's point of view, Latrice has a pink background, though in reality her walls were painted a warm shade of grey with a hue of caramel brown. Lord knows the guy at Home Depot took the time to get the mixture just right.

Whatever, what's important is that right now Latrice wants to find a true connection so that she could feel comfortable in revealing some of her sexiness. She's sick of not getting any attention. And this shadowy man is just one more layer of frustration that Latrice will have to work through. But she can't get but so frustrated.

"Come on girl, think clearly."

Many rainy days and weeks have gone by without a special someone paying Latrice the attention that she needs. And even though Asani is coming out as a shadow, he hasn't moved his body in the last five minutes. And Latrice realizes that her thoughts are becoming more focused.

And then Latrice asks, "Why are you all quiet over there? What you doin'?"

When she knows good and well what Asani is doing. "Uh uh. You better not be over there..."

Asani struggles to interject. "Huh?"

Latrice says, "Huh nothin'. What are you doing?"

Asani is discovering for the first time what a hard on is. He's getting uncomfortable in his chair. And Latrice knows it.

She smiles, "Stand up."

And catches Asani off guard, "What?"

And Latrice responds, "You heard me."

And Asani slowly stands up, slowly but surely.

She says, "Turn to the side."

And he does.

"Wow! Really? Like that" Latrice's eyes are glued to the screen.

And she mumbles, "You know what to do with all that? Mm."

And Kaylandria's voice says to Latrice, "Latrice, watch your thoughts."

Asani didn't hear that. "What did you say?"

"Nothing."

Oh but look at Asani's nice big fat hard-on. It looks like grey sweats or something that he has on. Her mouth cannot help but to get watery as she sees his penis poking out, as if needing to be noticed.

And then the screen goes back to being shadowy.

Kaylandria says, "Latrice."

"What? What. What!"

And then she realizes that this is new for him. "You know I've never done this whole internet thing before."

And Asani sits down. "Yeah, me too. Never done this before myself. What do they call you?"

Latrice smiles as she sits down and just loves the way that he just asked that question. "They call me Latrice."

And then there's this pregnant pause of silence. Latrice gets uncomfortable. "Well talk."

And that makes Asani uncomfortable. "About what?"

Perfect, just what Latrice needed, a guy who can't hold a conversation. "You know what? It was nice chatting but..."

But Latrice's voice is so different to Asani. He dares not let her go. "Your voice is different. Can you tell me a little about who you are?"

After letting that question fall on her, Latrice takes a second, and she says, "All I'm gonna tell you is, I am so easy to fall in love with."

Oh goodness. That sounded so incredibly nice and warm to Asani coming out of her mouth. It's as if she were reaching through the line and just enveloping him in a hug that just smothered his entire body, only leaving him room to breathe. They both enjoy the moment of supposing her moist full lips on his well-defined smooth cheek. Imagining her sitting on his lap, she weighs just enough, and is positioned just right on his upper thigh to where his blood is pushed back toward his genital area, allowing for legs to cross other legs, which causes her knee to gently rub up against the arrival of his new potential participant.

It's exactly what he needed to hear, and he says, "You give me the impression that you say things for a certain reaction."

"Is your intuition usually on point?"

"On what point?"

She smiles as she shakes her head, "Nothing. You judge for yourself. But don't say that I didn't warn you."

Asani is obviously smitten by the caressing of Latrice's soft and warm vernacular. He responds, "I see."

Latrice smiles. "And what is it that you see?"

Asani responds. "That you see what I see."

"So describe your life."

And it's not hard for Asani to articulate the proper response. "I don't know. I don't where I've been."

"What?"

"I don't know how I got here. But however I got here, I'm glad that I am here talking to you."

Curious and still comfortable, Latrice knows that he's probably just still turned on and it's hard for this mysterious dude to think straight. It makes her feel good nonetheless.

Asani asks, "Do you have any children?"

She could choke on her tongue she's so speechless, "Wow. Why in the world would he ask me that?

She hopes that by her not responding to that question that he might feel stupid for asking such a sensitive question about her. But she answers anyway, "No!"

Latrice's mind cannot help but to be pulled back to the loss of her child. Latrice sighs heavily into a hope that she may end up dying with.

Asani responds, "I can hear your thoughts."

Latrice smiles. "Oh really? Then what am I thinking?"

"I don't know. Maybe all of my thoughts are so loud that I think they're coming from you. You ever have the feeling that you were just getting to know yourself for the first time?"

Latrice sighs. "Yes. You have no clue."

Asani says, "I feel like I am caught between two places."

That is exactly what Latrice is experiencing right now, but she still asks, "What do you mean?"

"I have no clue, like I am being held somewhere, by something or someone."

Latrice says, "You want me to call the police? I mean I can hang up and call em' if you're being detained somewhere."

Asani replies, "Latrice."

Now she begins to wonder, "What's happening with you over there?"

Asani says, "Listen, I'm just sharing how I feel."

Latrice adds, "Oh. Okay. So where do you live again?"

Asani realizes that he has to answer this question with extreme caution. He thinks to himself, "Do I lie? Or do I say, 'I don't know'? Or should I ask Bowers to help me."

After two hard seconds of silence, Latrice asks, "Do you live with someone?"

More silence, but Asani answers, "Yes."

She pouts, "Male or female?"

And he responds, "Uh yeah, like me."

She laughs, "What do you mean 'like me'?"

Asani gets a little flustered and sighs. "Yeah, you may as well say I'm here alone. So when you're not doing this with me, what are you doing?"

It kind of takes Latrice out of her moment, but she doesn't mind so much. "Well, I'm in a little bit in transition right now. Well, I guess you can say I'm in the same place as you."

And Asani perks up. "Really?"

"Well, I'm sure I am not the exact same place. But you know, that feeling of being lost, like you don't know whether you belong here or there?"

Asani releases a sigh of joy and relief.

Latrice has her arms around her legs. As her heels allow her pretty toes to twinkle around, her chin rests neatly between her squareish kneecaps. "Yeah, I got kind of burned out on doing the whole corporate America thing. So I'm doing a little bit of soul searching right now. I've always liked uncovering things. I think I'm going to do something that I've always wanted to do, like take a trip to the motherland and do some digging. I mean literally get dirty and do some digging."

"Okay."

"I mean, I'm sure that a bunch of other people have been there. And it's not like I'm going to uncover anything new like a dinosaur or anything."

"Then why go?"

"Excuse me?"

"Why bother in going if you already know what the outcome is going to be?"

"That's not what I meant."

Asani is intrigued. "Ok, well, I don't know what the motherland is, but it sounds nice. Is that where your mother lives?"

Latrice laughs, "No. Is that where you mother lives?"

Asani stops to consider, "No."

He turns around and looks at his surroundings in the house. "I have no clue where my mother is. Where about do you want to search?"

Latrice's ear gets snagged, but she responds, "Uhm Egypt, but not just the typical ancient Egypt. I'm talking about the Egypt that Black folks speculate over, the place where no one else wants to believe existed."

Asani is intrigued. "Really? How long have you been interested in this? Wait. What is a Black folk?"

Latrice giggles in amazement, "Are you kidding? What color are you? There's no way in the world, I mean you sound Black. Are you Black?"

Asani gets a little annoyed. "What do you mean? Why do you call yourself a color?"

Latrice bites back a little, "Hey look, no need in getting all sensitive. That's just what we've always been called?"

And Asani responds, "By who?"

Latrice defends herself, "It's a name, I don't know, since the Civil Rights Movement, since slavery."

All of that snags Asani's ear now as he stands up. "Wait, what kind of movement? And when were you enslaved?"

Latrice gets a little concerned, "Don't tell me that you're one of these guys who doesn't acknowledge color? Where are you from, Martha's Vineyard?"

Asani just goes with it. "Okay, whatever you say. As long as you're okay. And no one is harming you. Are you in any danger?"

Latrice plays with the upper part of her warm ear as she smiles. "No. I'm fine. I'm a little worried about you though. Where did you say you were from?"

And Asani responds, "I don't think I did."

Latrice gets out of her chair. "Are you married? Cause if you are…"

Asani shields himself by putting his hands out in front of him and responds, "The only thing that I am married to is the idea of getting to know you."

And that shuts Latrice right on up.

Asani says, "Hello?"

Latrice says, "You just think that you know all the right things to say, don't you?"

And Asani liked that, the warmness of that interaction causes him to stumble in his thought, and he gets shy.

Latrice's eyes are shifting back and forth, looking for him. "Hello?"

"Yes?"

"Did I lose you?"

"That would be impossible to do."

The attention is something that he definitely isn't used to.

It's a beautiful and wonderful thing to be in a situation that has so much newness to it. Latrice definitely likes it. "I mean I ain't no dummy, but I don't get into anything that I can't wrap my mind around."

On the other end, Asani is doing his own rationalizing. "Yes, it is all new to me as well. Just about everything is new. I really look forward to getting to know you."

She's glad that Asani has taken interest in her. But she can't give in all the way, "That's what you say now."

Cн 30

And so after two hours, the conversation continues. The sun is nowhere to be found, and Latrice's laughter and guard coming down has her running to the bathroom, and she's thinking, "If I'm in this house or room, then why is my bladder still acting like its full?"

Kaylandria communicates to Latrice by way of thought, "Just because you're in the House of Erydia doesn't mean you don't need to pee."

"Fine." It's frustrating because she's discovered that she's out of toilet paper. And then she remembers that there is one emergency roll underneath the sink.

On the other end, Bowers has let the window up in the front room just a little, allowing for a slight breeze to come through his strange house.

He says to Asani as he waits on Latrice, "You still talking to her?"

And then she comes back. "Okay, I'm back. So you asked me what I like, right?"

Asani says, "Yes, what interests you?"

Latrice says, "I like ancient African studies.

Asani responds, "African."

Latrice continues, "Yeah, and not the stuff that you read about in the books but last year I had an opportunity to travel over to Africa."

In the better days of Latrice and Rick's relationship, they went to Egypt and found someone from the Dogon Tribe.

She says to Asani, "I got to take part of a pilgrimage that traced the steps through where an ancient civilization used to be."

But it was really Rick who wanted to go and fulfill this dream of his. Latrice could have went back to Bamako, but it was nine hours away by bus. And Rick was only going to be a few hours, so he says.

So Latrice is still talking to Asani, and she's beginning to really open herself up, saying, "It literally blew my mind. That tribe of people is seriously feared by people here. They know stuff that the best astronomers could never know."

Rick would be shaking his head right now if he heard his estranged spouse as he would easily say, "You didn't even want to go to Africa. I had to make you stay and not cut my trip short. You were afraid of the Cliff of Bandiagara, thinking that you were going to fall off.

But Latrice says to Asani, "And there's an entire philosophy that goes with their culture and lifestyle."

And Asani responds, "I'm sure. It's all about the culture and the study of the people."

There's a pause of silence and Latrice responds, "Uh yeah, sure."

She's carrying the conversation, and she thinks to herself, "I wish I could find someone who could make me feel more of what I want to feel."

He intuitively says, "Me too."

Latrice's eyelids flutter in disbelief. "What?"

And Asani confidently speaks. "You heard me. I know that you want me to connect with you, but you're speaking to me in terms of a place that you know I've never been."

She's intrigued once more. "Continue."

And he does, "Well, you're talking about a tribe of people who have locked away valuable information, information that has been passed down from millennia to millennia."

And Bowers, from out of nowhere pulls him from out of his seat. "What do you call yourself doing? Whatever you think you know, you need to not be sharing it with strangers."

Asani pushes him off of him. "Don't you touch me!"

And Bowers tries another tactic, "Look, you don't have anything to prove to her."

Asani gets back in front of the computer. "I think it would be a good idea for us to go there and take a look at this place in Mali right, the Cliff of Bandiagara Escarpment."

Latrice is startled, "Wow, how did you know?"

"I don't know. I just know."

Latrice is admiring the pretty tall yellow tulips on her computer desk. "Okay, so I'm not going to ask you where you live again. And I'm not going to ask you about your living arrangement. I'm just going to trust you. Can I do that?"

"Yes you can."

"Are you sure?"

Asani has no clue what he's agreeing to but he responds, "I said yes."

"Okay, so you're gonna meet me here? What's your plan?"

And Asani responds, "Don't worry. We'll figure it out when I get there."

Latrice places the flowers down by her side. "And when will that be? You know what? I'm sorry. Part of me believes that you won't come. So we'll see."

But Latrice has another issue to settle. She knows that the situation between her and Rick has not been resolved.

And in that instant, the conversation ends Asani fades out. Latrice cannot hear a thing. And the darkness takes hold of her comfy work area. The warm carpet turns to something that feels like ice cold needles, causing Latrice to stand up in her chair. But then the chair begins to break, causing Latrice to scream.

Cн 31

She gets interrupted by a receptionist in an office. "Latrice Foster? Dr. Vincent will see you now."

She thinks, "Should I just turn around and go call him". She does. "Okay, give me a moment."

Latrice knows that the house has pushed her out of what she knows as her own space and into the dark operating room again. This time she knows that she needs to pull her phone out of her purse and dial her estranged husband's number.

Latrice lets out a scream, "Do not make me experience this again!"

She knows that Kaylandria is listening, but this time she says not one word. And it makes Latrice begin to feel tortured, as if she has no choice but to allow this to play out once more.

She hears the phone ringing. Her eyes have no idea where to look. It doesn't matter. What she needs to see isn't coming into focus.

Latrice goes to voice mail. "You've reached the voice mail of Rickland Foster..." She bypasses the greeting. "You know who this is. You can call me back or not. I don't care."

The assistant peaks her head through her window. "Mrs. Foster..." Latrice sees herself past into the back.

Dr. Vincent smiles. "Well the good news is that your body is in fantastic shape. You have the blood sugar, weight, and heart of a twenty-five year old."

Latrice shakes her head slightly. "I already know what you're gonna say."

Then Dr. Vincent speaks, "The really bad cramping..."

Latrice looks up to the ceiling as she does not want to even look at this woman. She releases her clinched teeth. "I aint' trying to hear all of this from you! Kaylandria, get me out of here, right now!"

Kaylandria's voice says, "I brought you here to learn one thing and one thing only, someone has deceived you."

Latrice can hear her but it's not like she can do anything about it. Her actions are a slave to this scheduled exchange.

Dr. Vincent takes her black framed glasses off of her nose as a bead of sweat begins to materialize on the first of many forehead wrinkles. She then interjects, "And that we needed to keep a close eye on everything."

Kaylandria says, "Who you have known as Dr. Vincent is really an alien agent of darkness."

Dr. Vincent tries to hold her patient's hand but Latrice snatches it away, scratching the outside of Dr. Vincent's palm with her sharp nails. Latrice notices that she does not even bleed.

Kaylandria says, "Who you believe you know, you must know even better. For your life as already been targeted. The essence of the real Dr. Vincent is imprisoned somewhere else in the very deep recess of another universe. Five is clever. He can take on the form of just about any human, all except the First Family. He can also manipulate thoughts within the human brain."

Latrice responds in thought while still in the presence of Dr. Vincent, "Well, what can I do about this, Five? Why was my baby targeted?"

Kaylandria continues, "What you must know is that your miscarriage was all part of a plan, a war being waged far away from this planet between good and evil. His Master on my home timeline is Onjito. But Five, also serves under Gonondrius, each one just as evil as the previous. But Five's most earnest desire is to be free."

"Hell, don't we all. I remember this visit with Dr. Vincent. It was after Rick rushed me to the hospital. It was all so fast. So she's not really Dr. Vincent, but someone else?"

"That is correct."

Latrice then looks on as she sees herself interact with this Dr. Vincent in her office.

Dr. Vincent continues on to say, "Okay let's try to look at the bright side of this, because I have more good news. You are going to ovulate between now and your next cycle. I know this is hard and difficult, but you are your most fertile right now. So you and Rick should have a talk and when you're heart says yes you two should try again."

But Latrice's not having it. She just shakes her head a couple of times and steps in for a closer look. And then Latrice grabs Dr. Vincent by her shoulders and looks deep into her eyes.

"I don't know who you are but you're not Dr. Vincent."

Dr. Vincent tries to hold her hand again, but Latrice doesn't allow for it.

Latrice just looks at this shell of Dr. Vincent as it makes her skin crawl with so much anger.

Kaylandria says, "You want to hit her don't you?"

Latrice responds, "You have no clue."

"Then go ahead."

"Go ahead and what?"

"Hit her."

"I'm not going to hit her."

"But you can. Do it."

Instead, Latrice grabs her purse, and comes to the green door and pushes the cold handle down to open, and she interjects, "When something isn't possible, I am learning to do better about just moving on."

And then Latrice finds herself back in the House of Erydia, standing outside of the first room. The door closes on its own.

And Kaylandria's voice says, "All of that for nothing. Just lock the door."

Latrice finds the set of keys and she manages to lock the door. She makes sure that the knob doesn't twist, and the door does not open. And before her very eyes, the door to that room disappears, leaving something in its place. Latrice cannot believe it. The amazing yellowish hue portrait found in Latrice's very own home has now taken the place of the strange door.

Latrice says, "So Kaylandria, where are you now?"

"I don't think you want to know."

"I asked, didn't I?"

"Well, right now I am learning how to care for my child, the new universe that I just birthed."

Latrice sighs.

"I'm sorry."

Latrice says, "You're crazy.   And I'm even crazier for allowing any of this to happen."

"You do have a choice. You can either stay or go back."

"I know better than that. Staying here, although I have no clue as to what's going to happen, it beats just sitting at home."

Kaylandria voice says, "To the right."

And Latrice looks down the hallway and sees the next door. She walks toward the door and takes out her keys. And then all of a sudden, a dense mist in the form of a woman's body rushes Latrice from behind

and overtakes her, making Latrice sleepy and fall softy
to the floor.

Ch 32

Latrice opens her eyes and discovers that she's somehow back in her own bed.

"Latrice?"

"It couldn't be", Latrice thinks.

Shonnie comes in the bedroom. "Hey."

"How did I get here?"

"Oh, you are trippin'. Are you kidding? You came to my house looking all crazy about thirty minutes ago."

Latrice responds as she tries to sit up in the bed, "Shut up, and why you got me all under the covers like it's time to go to bed."

Shonnie is walking barefoot towards her closet in the room where she's placing her extra bath towels which are still very warm from the dryer. "You parked in the middle of the street and left the car in neutral."

Still clothed and with a cool folded bath cloth on her forehead, Latrice says. "No."

"You better be glad my neighbor recognized you."

"Oh no."

"How did you end up parking your car in the middle of the street, and then walk to my front door?"

Latrice says, "No. No. No."

"He wanted to call an ambulance, but I wouldn't let him."

"Oh my god. I don't believe this. Wow."

"Girl, you better be glad I was home. Where were you coming from?"

"Huh? Oh. Kaylandria's house, Erydia."

"Did you bump your head?"

Cʜ 33

Shonnie drives Latrice back in her white Ford Explorer to where she was. "Turn this corner."

"Huh? Did you turn on the wrong street?" Latrice turns and looks over her shoulder in confusion.

"It was…"

Shonnie just looks ahead with her lips in a little frown as Latrice tries locating the house by trying to point it back into place, but it's not there.

"This is the house, I mean the place… the place where that house was! It was right here!"

Shonnie is leaned forward over the steering wheel and looking at her like she is absolutely crazy. "Latrice."

Latrice unbuckles her seat belt. "No. I know what I'm talking about. Wait here."

Shonnie puts the car in park.

Latrice comes onto the inclined front yard of what should be Kaylandria's house.

She thinks, "Impossible, the house is gone."

There is a house, but it's an ugly forest green one-story house.

Latrice stands on the same steps, same sidewalk with her hands pressed hard on her hips. She sighs. "It was right here."

A strange but nice little lady in her 70's walks up and responds "What was here?"

Latrice turns around and looks at her with a scrunched up face. She leans in a little and acts like she wants to touch her but she doesn't dare.

"Kaylandria?"

"Who? No. My name is Robin... Stallings. Are you with the post office?"

"No."

"Because I'm getting mail that doesn't belong here."

"What's your name?"

Latrice's head is obviously somewhere else.

"Hello?"

"Oh, Latrice."

"Yes. I have a letter for you. Well come on in with me."

Latrice hesitates.

"Well I'm not going to bite or kidnap you."

Latrice follows Ms. Stallings into the whimsical little house. And sure enough, the house is so different, even in just comparing the first floors.

Shonnie backs up and parks the car under a very cool shady tree. She reclines the seat back and looks at her dash and the time reads, "3:37 PM".

Ms. Stallings says, "Ah, here it is. One letter addressed to Latrice Foster. And two keys. Do these belong to you?"

With her little frail Caucasian wrinkled hands with aging beauty marks, Ms. Stallings hands a large brown envelope to Latrice.

Latrice responds, "Oh, you've opened it."

She takes her large straw garden hat off and gets just a little indignant, shrugging her left shoulder, "Well, if I didn't open that letter, I wouldn't have known how urgent it was."

Latrice looks inside and pulls out two airline tickets and two keys.

Ms. Stallings gets right in Latrice's face, toe to toe, "Now those keys better not go to this house."

"Well, I don't know."

Ms. Stallings offers a loving smile, responding, "No they don't. I just checked. Probably to another house, but I don't know where. So don't ask."

Latrice examines each ticket.

"I believe it's dated for today. You know it's a good thing that you came by today. That letter's been sitting here since... since... well, I can't even remember.

Ms. Stallings goes into the kitchen and brings out a tray of iced cold tea in a very robust glass picture.

She leads Latrice onto the side of the strange green foresty house under an ivy covered trellis. "I can't even remember how long it's been here. And what did you say your name was?"

"Oh umm, Latrice, Foster."

"And do I know you? Oh, I'm sorry. You'll have to leave now. It's time for my nap."

"I'd better be going now. Thank you. It's been a pleasure."

Seventeen minutes has passed, and Latrice gets back in the car with Shonnie.

With her temple resting on the steering wheel, Shonnie says, "What was that all about?"

Latrice replies, "I don't understand. That house was right there."

Shonnie smirks. "I saw her give you something."

Latrice takes the tickets out of the envelope and looks at it. One airline ticket has all of Latrice's personal information, including address, phone number, the last four digits of her social security number, but it says, 'Time: TBD", and then second ticket was simply a credit of equal value. Latrice just shakes her head, trying to make sense of this. "Shonnie, you want to take a trip with me?"

Shonnie responds, "I guess. When?"

"Tomorrow."

"You have clothes to travel? Wait. First where are we going?"

"I don't know, maybe Brazil."

Shonnie says nothing.

"I'm going. Matter of fact, I'm already packed."

"Wait, what you mean you're already packed?

Shonnie says, "You know I keep a bag packed on standby. I just don't fly standby. Where your clothes?"

"I don't need any?"

"What you mean you don't need clothes?"

"I'll buy some."

"How long are we planning on staying? Where are we staying?"

"There's a house that I have to look for?"

"You have an address? Where's your passport?"

Latrice says nothing.

Shonnie, replies. "Rick has it?"

Ch 34

Later on in the coolness of the evening, Latrice makes the trek through the Hampton Roads Tunnel over to Hampton.

She climbs the deep pitched concrete steps that lead her to the front door. And she attempts to ring the doorbell but Rick opens just before she does. "How did you find me?"

He hides in the shadow in the foyer. "Close the door."

Latrice responds, "It wasn't hard. I knew you either had to be at your mom or your brother's, and since your brother is out of the country, I figured I'd start here."

Latrice didn't really plan on looking at him, but since he's being standoffish, she says, "Why are you… what's wrong… what happened to you?"

Latrice is noticing that Rick's body has somehow changed. "I mean like damn. What happened to you?"

Rick walks around mostly with shades on, but Latrice knows how he walks around when he's got something on his mind.

"Listen I'm not here to say anything. But the stuff that you packed in my box, how come I didn't see that stuff I need?"

"What stuff?"

Latrice just looks at him. "What's wrong with you? What you got shades on in the house for?"

"How bout my eyes hurt, if that's okay with you."

She says, "What? I'm just asking. I put everything in different boxes."

Latrice takes the liberty to go through the house. "I know."

"Look. What are you looking for?"

"I need my birth certificate."

"I put that..."

"No you didn't."

"Did you look…"

"I wouldn't have driven here had I not."

So Rick walks Latrice through the house to the empty dining room where all the boxes are.

Rick says, "It might be in there."

Latrice gets on her knees and opens the box up with the Exacto Knife on her key ring, making Rick back up quickly.

"Well it's not."

"Try…"

"What does it look like I'm doing?"

"Trying."

"That's right I'm trying."

"I can see that."

"Good."

Latrice continues searching, not really caring about how anything else is arranged in the box.

"You know what? I'm sorry. Did I say birth certificate?"

"Yes."

"I'm sorry. I meant to say I'm looking for my passport."

"Okay."

She is on the fourth box, and she finds the passport. She gets up from off of her knees.

Rick says, "I mean, are you gonna pick all of this back up? Don't worry about it."

Latrice starts silently darting for the door.

Rick says, "So where are you going?"

She says nothing, and goes for her keys.

"Did you hear what I asked?"

"Yes."

He says, "I just needed a little space."

"Good."

Rick didn't expect Latrice to come over lookn' all good. The obvious moment that he's trying to figure out what to say is prolonged as he is reminded, "Damn Latrice is fine."

Rick says, "Maybe we should take some time, to talk about this... you know?"

Latrice responds, "Maybe not."

"You still never told me where you're going."

Latrice goes for the door. "And I still haven't."

But Rick extends his long strong arm at the top of the door. "You're still my wife."

It's almost laughable that Rick is trying to prevent her from leaving. "You are in my way."

"No I'm not. You can leave."

"And when did you start wearing leather bracelets?"

Rick rolls his eyes. "Listen. You think you're the only one hurting from the miscarriage?"

"I don't want to hear this."

Rick sighs, "This is something we both have to deal with."

She tries opening the door once more. And in the process, a little rubbing happens. Latrice knows that he'll probably reach out and touch her ass, but he thinks better. Instead he just looks into her eyes.

Latrice responds, "It's not working.

Rick says, "Look, I know that I've been closed off. I made it so you couldn't get to me.

"Listen, I'm good."

So Rick starts to takes his sunglasses off and exposes his eyes, but he changes his mind.

Latrice opens the front door and she closes the door behind herself, and Rick does not follow.

CH 35

The next morning at 11, Latrice arrives at the airport with Shonnie at the wheel, and in haste she manages to get to the airport with barely an hour before the flight takes off.

Latrice is sitting in the passenger seat annoyed. And Shonnie says, "You annoyed cause you ain't get none."

"Shut up."

Shonnie says, "I'm just saying, you got all that 'I want sex with my ex' energy all up in my front seat."

Latrice shoots Shonnie a look.

"I keep my passport in my purse."

"Along with a super pack of condoms."

"Meet My King baby. Don't hate, cause me and Esteban hookin' up when we land."

They park and walk in with one shoulder bag a piece.

Shonnie says, "Now how in the world are you gonna have enough clothes?"

"I don't know. I'm just gonna wing it."

"Wing it. Great."

"If I need clothes, I'll just buy some."

Latrice's choices are being observed from afar. One says to another, "If he goes with her to South America in modern day, all is over." And the Creator's voice replies, "But Kaylandria, if he does not go with her, then she will still proceed."

Shonnie and Latrice walk into the terminal.

The ladies come into the airport and start their process of checking in. But a few dozen feet away on a set of steps, pretending like he's reading a pamphlet, is Rick.

They get their tickets.

They go through TSA.

Latrice walks through the scanner first, and the scanner detects nothing.

After Shonnie comes through the scanner, Latrice sees that just a couple of people behind her is Rick. "Girl, why is Rick over there in those sun glasses? Is that his idea of a disguise?"

An overweight TSA officer on his first day of work gets a little skeptic and goes over to Rick. "Sir, please remove your shades."

Rick responds, "There's no metal in these shades?"

"You heard me."

Rick says, "And you heard me."

The overzealous TSA worker, who barely passed his test to get hired, says, "I'm going to have to ask you to step over here."

Rick is thrown off by his lack of professionalism and says, "I beg your pardon."

Fueled with tense emotion, Rick does not think and decides to use his new bracelet. But just as he begins to utter the phrase to activate its power, his tongue gets tied. Rick trips over his own words.

He hears the words from Arah back in his lab, "The bracelet is already limited in power. If you use it just once, you will cease to exist here and lose all memory of this time. The bracelet, according to the will of the Creator, will then take itself and its bearer to its source."

And the TSA guard yells, "Sir. Hand it over, the glasses and that bracelet!"

Another officer comes up from behind and snatches the glasses off of Rick's face.

And Latrice sees Rick's eyes, completely transparent, as if she could see directly into the recesses of an unfamiliar soul. She thinks, "Something happened to him."

Then Latrice says, "What are you doing? He's just pulling out his ID!"

A TSA Officer turns to Latrice. "Move back!"

Latrice gets pushed to the side.

Another officer says to Rick, "Place your hands above your head and don't move."

Latrice says, "Look at his ID. He's… "

Latrice turns around as if she's going to take up for Rick. But she doesn't because the officer that's closest to her is trying to detain him, and he turns to Latrice. "Come here."

Rick sees it, and yells, "Hey…"

Then Latrice raises her hands and she is scanned.

"The computer finds something on Rick."

Kaylandria then speaks into the mind Latrice, "You must not interfere."

Another officer says to Latrice, "Do you have a flight to catch?"

Latrice says, "Yes, but look. What has that man done?"

A cop slaps the cuffs on Rick and he is taken by the other TSA officers into a back room.

The leader of that team of officers speaks switches walkie channels and says, "We have him."

That news brings much pleasure to one who has also survived for several eternities, Gonondrius, the current master along this time line on another side of the Perimeter with whom Five has chosen to serve in promise of partnership. It is through Five's efforts that brings this dark ruler and native son of the Earth one step closer to realizing his self-determined purpose.

"If all goes according to my plan, then the Earth and its people will relinquish its holding place in my solar system of stars. And I will not need a path in which to travel because I will have in my possession the Rods of the Yeswe'. And the first step in getting the Rods is having the bracelet of the Urangule', which I now have in my possession. Isn't that correct?"

Five says while standing alongside a porthole that is now closing up on his space vessel, "I am in the process of gathering the rods now."

But what Gonondrius does not know is that Five has already begun reclaiming the Rods.

Gonondrius says, "I am allowing you to execute this plan because I know that you know if you fail me, you know that I would not look upon that too favorably. You know that don't you?"

In his patronizing subservient tone, Five responds "I assure you. Our plan will come to pass."

"I know. I grow weary and I am homesick. And I will finally have the bracelet that was always intended for me to have. And the son of my foolish brother hasn't any idea what is happening."

Being tended to by female species from other worlds, Gonondrius looks down from his chair onto Five. "Whatever you are doing, just do not disappoint me."

"You should have more faith in your partner."

"Why have faith when you can simply just believe in me?"

Five creates a porthole and disappears.

CH 36

Meanwhile back inside Norfolk International Airport which is now on alert, an officer says to a frantic Latrice, "I would advise you, if you want to get to your destination…"

Just as he says that, Latrice gets distracted and she sees a woman on the runway. She cannot believe her eyes. "Is that Kaylandria?"

There's a call coming in on the radio. "He's secured."

Latrice says, "Why are you holding him. His name is Rickland Foster? We have a flight to catch!"

And then Latrice looks back and sees that she left Shonnie back in the line. "Latrice, you got my ticket! I can't get through the line."

Latrice has a decision to make. "Do I grab Shonnie and pull her through the scanner? Or do I save the ticket for Rick and see what's going on with him? Or do I not do anything and just stand here?"

The officer responds, "Ma'am, you have to do something. You can't just stand here."

Latrice thinks about it.

Shonnie begins walking in the opposite direction. "I'm gone."

Latrice yells back, "Shonnie wait!"

Shonnie is out and she's talking under her breath. All you can really hear are her squeaky flip flops. "Ole' big head, she knows I cannot stand flakey people."

Shonnie gets a tap on her shoulder. She turns around and it's another TSA officer, a very rugged hunky one at that. And he hands her the ticket. "Your friend was trying to hand this to you but you were moving away too fast."

Latrice watches Shonnie head to her gate. "She's gonna kill me."

And Shonnie yells to Latrice, "That's cool. See how you do your maid of honor? We'll talk when I get back!"

Latrice sighs and then an officer says to her, "I believe your gate is right over there."

Latrice's eyes scan the room quickly, and there's her gate. A dressed-to-the-nine ticket agent is standing at the gate, all alone, with an inquisitive smirk on her face, tapping on the glass of her wrist watch. "We've been waiting for you Mrs. Foster."

Rather slowly, Latrice makes her way over to her gate.

The ticket agent says, "Come on. We don't have that much time."

Latrice responds, "What are you talking about? There's no plane."

The happy-go-lucky ticket agent says, "Oh Latrice. Get a move on."

Latrice walks to the edge of the tarmac. She almost falls to the ground below. And that's a good sixteen feet down. "Where the hell is the plane?"

Kaylandria speaks directly into her thoughts, "Allow me to show you a way that was once long ago shown to me."

The skies are stricken with heavy overcast clouds.

The airport sits right on the coastline. And then piercing out of the bay, a massive dark menacing steel-plated bridge quickly emerges off the Virginia coast, where the Chesapeake Bay meets the Atlantic Ocean. The bridge's appearance is so intimidating.

Latrice loses her bag in the wind, with the airport slowly fades away into a cloudy mist. And she says, "Where in the world did all of this come from?"

Kaylandria responds, "Only your feet may grace this path. For another to do so, will render this path inoperative."

It's tall and terrifying, but at the same time, it is beautiful. Latrice marvels at this intimidating creation. "Who in the world made this?"

She takes one step from the edge of the airport runway, and the menacing bridge disappears. And her foot is gripped. Latrice screams. Some strange force is keeping her body from being hurled into the aggressive Atlantic Ocean. It's not even hurricane season.

Kaylandria's voice says, "You are on the path as long as you believe."

Latrice is in straight shock and responds, "For how long?"

Latrice cannot believe that she's moving in the manner in which she is. It's incredible, the speed, the effortlessness, the freedom.

"But where am I going?"

Kaylandria's voice says, "You are now traveling over the vastness of what is now the Atlantic Ocean."

And in that moment, Latrice's body comes to a complete stop. She is in midair, completely motionless. She's scared stiff as she contemplates what the hell lies beneath the now watery surface.

Latrice looks around in every direction, hoping that Kayalndria is still somewhere close by. "Why have I stopped?"

She hears nothing. And for the next several hours, Latrice has remained in this position.

"Why did you leave him behind?"

"What?"

"Just curious."

Latrice is annoyed as that conjures up feelings of her being recently abandoned. "He'll be fine. He has his credentials. And if he does not, they'll figure it all out."

"Really? You miss him don't you?"

Latrice remembers some of their more precious moments, making love on a Sunday morning in the calmness of another one of their previous homes. She gets upset and says to Kaylandria, "I thought I was supposed to be learning about the second story of a house."

Kaylandria responds, "I did say that, didn't I?"

Latrice says, "Yes you did. How did I get here? I go back the next day and the house is gone. And then I'm here, in the middle of the Atlantic freaking ocean, looking for who knows what! Where is the house? And where are you?"

"The house is exactly where you found it. As a matter of fact you are still in the house."

"No way. How?"

"Turn around."

And Latrice does. A door materializes. It opens. "I see a hallway."

The voice of Kaylandria says, "See."

Latrice adds, "And that hallway takes me out. I want out. How do I get out?"

Kaylandria says, "Don't you even want to know who built the bridge?

Latrice's heart beat is faster than normal and she begins to fatigue. "No. I did not ask you who built it."

"Fine. Someone goes to the great length to bring you all the way into their home, into places you've never been..."

Latrice says to pacify. "Okay, all right. Who built the bridge?"

"And the house."

"Wonderful! You built the house and now the bridge!"

"Remember, the bridge is inside the house."

"Why?"

"Why what?"

Latrice is annoyed, puffing her cheeks as she sighs. "Why is the bridge inside the house?"

Kaylandria responds. "You are on the Bridge of Soma, a bridge that was built long ago by an ancient race of people."

Latrice says, "Okay well let me off of the bridge, and let me get home, and you can tell me the rest."

"I am sorry. Once you leave the bridge you are not permitted to know any more."

Latrice picks up her left foot.

Kaylandria says, "The choice will always be yours."

Latrice remains. "What choice do I really have?"

Latrice takes a step backwards.

Kaylandria says, "In the House of Erydia, backwards sometimes means going forward."

And then yards away, a coastline appears behind Latrice. She turns around.

Latrice just stands there a shakes her head in awe, "Where I am? No, I mean what is this?"

Kaylandria responds, "Where you are now is what was once the Kingdom of Soma, or what is now called Chile'?"

"Kingdom? But that's impossible. I'm in the middle of the Atlantic."

Kaylandria says, "Now take a step in this direction."

Latrice steps forward. And the bridge does something perplexing. Latrice notices, "The Bridge is collapsing."

At a slow pace, the bridge begins to slope downward toward the coastline. But the ferocious waves produce an extra slippery surface and Latrice has to balance herself to keep from slipping off.

"I'm slipping!"

Kaylandria responds, "Then don't slip."

Latrice says, "I can't swim."

Kaylandria says, "Listen, all you have to do is look straight ahead and imagine yourself on the beach."

But Latrice clutches onto the nearby rail.

Kaylandria says, "You have to let go. Exercise your imagination."

"How?"

"You hold on to too much. Let it go."

And so in a flash of the sun's ray, Latrice arrives on the beach. "But where am I?"

Kaylandria responds, "Soma."

Latrice says, "But that cannot be. According to the direction, the speed, I should be somewhere else in Africa if anywhere.

Kaylandria rebuts, "Ah, but you are not. And what can you do about it?"

"Oh I'm a do something about it all right. You're going to tell me where I am."

"I am not. Now, I will tell you where you are not."

Kaylandria appears and looks around. She's dressed in an off-white something that puts the finest silk to shame. It flows so nicely on her elderly body. "I forgot how beautiful and interesting this place is."

Latrice says, "Well if you're not going to tell me where I am, how about telling me why I'm here."

"Oh, no you don't. Just take it as it comes. And the first part is coming to you right now."

Kaylandria has Latrice levitating as she moves forward into the thickest and loveliest rainforest leaves ever seen. Even the color of this air seems to have taken on a beautiful hue of mint green. "Look around Latrice. What do you see?"

There are the most adorable insects, the most delightful butterflies that dance around Latrice's body as if they've always known her. She holds her finger out and one lands, waving its wings as if it were saying, "Hello."

And that makes Latrice feels welcomed, allowing her to breathe a long sigh of relief and comfort. "I have never seen this before. Everything looks so new, like it's never been touched."

Kaylandria responds, "Exactly. You are here to witness the unfolding of the Earth's first civilization."

"Shut the front door." That's Latrice's way of saying, "Shut the hell up."

"I did. If you want me to open it again so you can go home..."

Latrice says to Kaylandria, "That was a figure of speech."

Ch 37

"**W**hat you are experiencing is somewhat of an alternate reality, made available to you for you to be exposed to the truth."

That truth is the past history of the Earth. This truth is now in place where it must express a desire to be known, felt, embraced, sheltered, and nurtured.

Latrice responds, "So all of this is in the house that I took you to where you had the baby… universe?"

Kaylandria then says, "Do you miss your child?"

Latrice wants to slap the mess out of Kaylandria. She takes a step forward. "Where ever I am, take me back."

"I can't."

"You will."

"I cannot."

Latrice goes and runs towards the water and throws her hands up into the air. "Bridge, appear!"

But nothing happens. "I say appear!"

Latrice goes further into the water, taking her mega step of faith into the air, but she splashes face down onto nothing but salt water.

Kaylandria looks on. And then she walks forward into the water. "You are here, with me."

Latrice arises drenched, like a wet Memphis cat, and wipes the stinging salt water from her face. And when she does, she expects to see Kaylandria.

"Who are you?"

"I beg your pardon."

Latrice opens her eyes and sees a beautiful younger woman before her. "Who are you?"

"Latrice, it's me, Kaylandria."

"But you're, younger, a whole lot younger! Wow. But how?"

Kaylandria is now much more youthful in her appearance and very beautiful with a slender feminine athlete's form. She dives into the somewhat choppy water and streaks around underwater like a nimble porpoise, taking a rather long circular route over to Latrice. She comes up out of the water without making a splash, and somehow in the process was able to remain dry. The smoothness of her skin is such a radiant shade of dark golden brown. Latrice was staring at Kaylandria much like a man would as he admired the most beautiful woman.

She walks Latrice onto dryer land, under a long shady palm whose rubbery form has taken the form of a convenient place to recline, much like a beach chair. The young sun is still very warm, but it's on the verge of setting.

Cн 38

After sunset, Latrice says, "I'm just so glad not to be in that mess of a relationship any longer. I took as much as I could."

They're both sitting on the beach. Kaylandria is a little fidgety, making shapes in the dry but still warm sand. "So you had enough of him?"

Latrice responds, "Uh yeah. I mean I can't tell you how much I appreciate you pulling me into this house. I still can't figure this out, but thank you. Have you ever felt like you needed to just get away, and figure out who you are?"

Such a touching question renders Kaylandria speechless. She sits next to Latrice leaning on the sand with one arm smiling and says, "What do you think

Rickland was trying to say to you at the airport? Oh I mean the night before."

Latrice responds, "What do you mean? Huh?"

"Think."

"I don't know."

"I believe you heard him, but you didn't necessarily care about connecting with him."

Latrice is annoyed, "Feel what? He said what he had to say and so did I. How do you know?"

Latrice remembers. "Oh. That's right, I'm in your house."

Kaylandria cautiously grabs Latrice's hands.

And right before her very eyes, Latrice is back inside of Rick's house and she sees herself arguing with Rick.

Latrice can see their mouths moving. "I can't hear."

Kaylandria interrupts, "Shhh, listen."

Latrice blinks her eyes in frustration. "I don't..."

Kaylandria responds, "Wait. Listen."

It's confusing. Rick's mouth is saying little to nothing, but Latrice is all of sudden bombarded with the voice of his thoughts. "I am pursuing something that is not within my grasp. I decided to dedicate my life towards a cause that cannot seem to find its way to me. But the call is strong nonetheless. Either I'm a fool for my choices, or there is a cause which needs fighting. So I go from always being a recipient to being sacrificed for a cause. I walk a path of accessing myself daily as a man, and fending off those who choose to devalue me. I do not know what has happened, but all I desire is to treat people with kindness and thoughtfulness. And maybe somewhere in my rationale that is the cost of respect. I am a man. And somewhere from the beginning of time til now, I wrestle. Something has been lost. I so feel extremely misunderstood. Something is missing."

And then Latrice finds herself back on the beach in front Kaylandria. "Don't you ever do that again!"

Kaylandria responds, "What did he mean by all of that?"

"I don't know. And I do not care. That is over! It's done! I don't want to think about that again."

Kaylandria says, "You can leave if you want. But if you do, your new connection will be severed, forever. You know of who I speak."

Ch 39

Still sitting on the beach under what is now the best of any deep purple hazy night, the strange mystical Kaylandria extends her hand towards the moon and directs a soft portion of its light onto the beach where they sit. Kaylandria says to Latrice, "Here in the House of Erydia you may think as great or as limited as you desire."

"I was wondering how this whole place worked. I mean this ain't no house... not my house anyway, you know what I mean."

So Latrice takes a look around her and there's nothing but beauty that she can still see glowing in the pitch dark of night. "So what can I do?"

Reclined on the sand without a care in the world, Kaylandria sits with her legs crossed and looks up at Latrice. "Use your imagination. What needs to be done?"

Latrice responds, "I think I want to do some exploring. I want to see. I want to build another bridge. But is there any way... I'd like to say hello to someone. This is gonna sound crazy but does this place... is there wi-fi somewhere around here?"

Kaylandria responds, "You have all the connection you need while you're in the house."

Latrice is excited and cannot get the words off of her tongue. "Right, right, right, right, right. Okay, so how do you connect with someone if you don't have a computer."

Kaylandria sits up playfully and goes to scooting herself behind Latrice, putting her arms around Latrice's waist. "Come here. Sit down. Be still. Feel your surroundings."

Latrice has her arms out a little cautiously thinking, "Okay, what are you doing?"

Then she slowly reaches out to touch and examine her breasts. "Yours are bigger than mine."

"Do not do that again."

Kaylandria pulls Latrice's hair back in a very neat ponytail. She makes sure that every hair is in place. And Latrice finds herself enjoying it a little.

Kaylandria asks, "Wait. Who is this that you'll be reaching out to?"

"I thought you said that you knew. I knew you weren't all knowing."

Kaylandria pauses and nudges Latrice on her back. "Hmm. You better hope I remembered to pay the bill."

Latrice says as her eyes are filled with so much life, "Pay what bill, to whom? All of this is still unbelievable. And you, where did you come from?"

It's very interesting what Latrice sees in Kaylandria. It's as if she was acting like a little child, and a bratty one at that.

"Yes. All connections cost. Now sit still. Close your eyes. And whoever this person is, think of... him."

Latrice sits comfortably with her eyes closed, but says nothing. She smiles as she knew that Kaylandria was fishing for information.

Kaylandria continues. "Think of the person. Think of the person. Think of the person. Speak with your mind. Speak with your mind. And again, speak with your mind. Your words are... his words. Your words are his words. Your words are his words."

Latrice finds her mind wondering into a calm and peaceful space. "It's so beautiful."

Her eyes are closed but they are open. "It's as if I am a part of everything."

Kaylandria responds, "That's good."

But Kaylandria senses that something does not feel right. "Now concentrate... on him."

And then Asani's voice is heard, "Hello."

Latrice responds, "Hi."

Kaylandria is a little surprised, but she shouldn't be.

Latrice says, "I can see you smiling."

Kaylandria is ready to back up and give her some space, but is completely pulled in by the smile on Latrice's face.

Kaylandria is a being who cannot help but to notice changes in behavior. With the casual wave of her hand, Kaylandria severs their connection. "Okay, that's enough."

Asani, on the other hand, is sitting in the darkness of his strange living room in front of his computer with the same confused look on his face. The weak light over the computer seems to be dying for some reason. Bowers comes running into the room. "You messin' with my light?"

Meanwhile, Latrice is kicking and screaming in the sand, "What did you just do? How are you just gonna cut my conversation?"

Kaylandria gets up with no need to wipe the gritty sand off her legs. She's disappointed as she sighs a little. "We have a lot of ground to cover."

"Ground? What ground?"

"We cannot stay here. If we do not move we will miss it."

Latrice responds, "Well, can I at least give him a call back? I want to let him know where I am."

Kaylandria responds, "Do you know where he is?"

"No."

"Do you even know how you're able to talk to him?"

"No."

"Do you want to talk to him again?"

"Yes."

"Well then I suggest you keep up with me. Anyway, you cannot talk to him for long periods of time."

Latrice is pissed and does not believe what Kaylandria just said, "Long periods of time, huh?"

Kaylandria knows that if she spent too much time talking, Asani's location would be discovered by the enemy. "Listen. No more questions. I will let you know when it is okay to speak with… what did you say his name was?"

Latrice responds, "I do not remember."

"You don't know? You're talking to someone you don't…"

"Yes, I know his name. It's Hassan."

Kaylandria says, "It is not."

Latrice fixes her mouth to ask a question, but she hesitates.

Ch 40

The next morning, Latrice wakes up to Kaylandria standing over her and saying, "Stay focused. And keep up."

Latrice responds, "The sun ain't even up yet."

"The sun never goes down."

Latrice has no choice to but to follow Kaylandria on foot into the wetness of this strange and moist tropical forest. "Wait up!"

And meanwhile, Asani is still in front of the computer, punching the keys, trying to figure out, "How was she able to reach out?"

Asani doesn't want to, but he just gives up because he's sleepy, and just flips the flimsy black switch down to turn the computer off.

He gets up and goes over to Bowers, who is leaning on the wall watching.

Bowers stands there with a little smirk.

Asani just walks by and goes down the hallway towards his bedroom.

Bowers goes outside, walking off into the darkness of the house. And Asani sneaks back to sit in front of the computer, hoping and wishing that he could touch her, somehow. He sighs, hoping to find the strength to hold onto her.

C_H 41

While the two women were trekking over the tall grassy plains on the other side of the tropical forest, they had conjured the curiosity of strange eyes from afar.

Kaylandria says to Latrice, "Another pair of eyes is trying to weigh upon us. We must move with haste."

For onboard of some strange sinister vessel, Five, second in command, comes in and speaks to a man, a ruler who lurks in the darkness of his own self-made abyss. His name is Gonondrius.

This ruler along this parallel universe says to the vertically challenged and somewhat frail Five, "Tell me that you have discovered Asani's whereabouts."

Ch 42

In another place, Latrice says to Kaylandria while traveling by foot over the marvelous terrain, "So while I am in this house, I have access to what?"

"My, aren't we just a little selfish?"

"Not at all. Just inquisitive. That's all."

Kaylandria stops walking for a second. "Knowledge... about things, people, dates, the past, the present, sometimes the future."

"I want to learn about someone."

"I know."

"Do you?"

"You sure can pick em'."

"Why do you say that?"

Kaylandria says, "His name is Asani. And right now, he is confused. He does not know where he is."

Latrice responds, "I see."

"One of the reasons that you are even here with me is because Asani found you."

"So he's lost."

"Not really, but yes."

"Well if you hadn't severed our connection, I might have been able to find out where he is."

"I don't need you to tell me where he is."

Latrice gets agitated, "Excuse me?"

"Where is your husband?"

"I have no clue."

They stand on a grassy hill near the edge of a desert.

Kaylandria says, "Well, I knew him and you before you knew yourselves. The reason that I severed your connection with Asani is because my power and capabilities draw attention. And it draws attention from individuals who mean Asani no good."

Latrice responds, "Yeah, but I thought we were in the house. Isn't this the all-powerful house with no limits, no limitations?"

Kaylandria closes her eyes, and the very ground beneath their feet begins to move, allowing them both to move just a few feet into the air, over the land, at a high velocity, in an eastward direction.

Latrice is getting dizzy, thinking of Rick's driving. "Wait. Stop. Where are we going?"

Kaylandria responds. "Lean forward."

Latrice leans forward and they both pierce through the wind, hair flying back out of their face.

Latrice says, "Can we slow down? My hair is whipping on my back."

"You should have kept it up in your ponytail."

And it was. The ends of Latrice's hair felt like sharp push pins being thrown at her upper back. Kaylandria rolls her eyes and slows their speed.

Kaylandria says, "In this world, everything is a function of when, time. Time spans here from your present all the way back to the beginning."

Latrice says, "Of time? When?"

Kaylandria responds, "Do you always think so linear? Everything is not always a straight line."

It's taking most of Latrice's attention to concentrate on flying.

Kaylandria rolls her eyes again. And she switches Latrice's position to one of sitting in an air-chair.

The grass, dirt, and other ground components tickle her feet. Nervously, she says, "It tickles."

Kaylandria sits as well, eyes closed, concentrating on where she wants to go. She knows exactly what the destination is.

Latrice says, "Uh, where are we going?"

"You're in the house. Remember?"

And Latrice just decides to be at peace for the moment and just take in the strange interior of the house. "How much time will it take for us to reach our destination?"

Kaylandria responds, "Time cannot be explained. It must be lived. Look around you. We are all the children of time. Feel the beauty around you. Allow your senses to reach out and fellowship with their surroundings. Here you are privy to an Earth that has not been for some time now."

Latrice realizes something. "What year is this?"

Kaylandria responds, "Wonderful question. We are going back to the beginning of time as you know it. This is why I impress upon you to open and free your mind. The House of Erydia works in tandem with the visitor's mind."

Latrice's ear gets snagged on the word Erydia.

Kaylandria continues, "The more that you are able to open your mind, the more of this world that you will be able to see."

As if it was hard enough already, Latrice has to open her eyes. "Why would you say that?"

Her thoughts are interrupted and her movement begins to stagger, and then Latrice falls onto the beginning of what looks like a desert.

But Kaylandria continues to move at her same speed. She waits for nothing. But her voice is still close to Latrice. "There is a layer of judgment that your mind has to break through in order for you to truly see."

Latrice bursts out. "You get back here right now! Why am I on this path? Why do I need to be here?"

Kaylandria's voice continues to speak though she is absolutely nowhere in sight. "The relevance of your path will display what you must see and learn."

And in her quiet space, Latrice begins to hear another voice. "No, it's two voices." She strains her closed eyes, clutching the sand with her somewhat dainty dry hands.

Kaylandria's voice can still be heard in a soft, faint whisper. "Be still, and listen. Let go."

Latrice is forced to inhale a large amount of air. It fills her body with a new understanding. She becomes confident and curious. She reaches out with her left hand. She's looking for something. She searches and without even thinking, Latrice wipes her hand across the sky and cuts her way into another space. She realizes that she's done something interesting and opens her eyes.

Still far away, Kaylandria's voice says, "No." And she mends together what Latrice just did.

Latrice breathes a sigh of understanding. "Whew, that was a little tiring."

Kaylandria's voice utters, "Keep your eyes closed Latrice. Find them."

Latrice is still sitting in the sand, eyes closed, arms extended, slightly bent, palms facing upward. She seems a little stiff though.

Kaylandria's voice says, "Relax Latrice. Relax."

Cн 43

Latrice's head moves to the left. She hears the two voices once more. "I hear something."

And with her eyes still closed, her thoughts say, "I see something."

Kaylandria says, "And what might that be?"

Latrice sees a blurry image of the House of Erydia. But when she goes through the front door, she sees another house. "A house… another one."

Kaylandria then says, "Open your eyes."

Latrice is shocked to discover herself outside of a rather plain 20th century one-story house.

Then a man appears. He comes outside the house to grab some fresh air and to stretch his limbs. And he begins to hear voices, Latrice and Kaylandria's.

Latrice expects Kaylandria to respond, but she says nothing.

"Kaylandria. Kaylandria!" Latrice scurries around the property looking for her, as if to will her into her sight. But it's just her, walking around the property looking pretty silly, trespassing on someone else's property."

But the man sees Latrice's shadow. And goodness look at the curves on her.

Whoever this man is, it's his first encounter with anything that looks like a woman. Latrice is all eyes and cannot see anything on herself other than her shadow.

He is standing there and he asks, "What's that?"

Just as Latrice is about to fix her mouth to answer, Kaylandria quietly says to her, "You cannot speak to him."

Latrice replies, "Well, why not?"

Kaylandria whispers, "I've already told you. If you do not obey my voice, then another voice will be introduced to you. Know my voice while you are not with me."

And in that instant, Latrice's mind puts it together. She begins mouthing to herself, almost actually saying aloud, "Asani?"

She doesn't want to get too excited, but she completely buys in to it whole heartedly. "Asani!"

Latrice starts fanning herself as she starts jumping around. She doesn't know what to feel. It's all so sudden and certainly unexpected. The essence of her girlish quality comes to visit and Latrice allows herself to obey Kaylandria. "Okay, okay. I'm sorry. But I can't believe it. Oh thank you Kaylandria. Thank you. Thank you. Thank you!"

In a very monotone uninterested voice, Kaylandria responds, "It is best to just observe."

Latrice realizes that this House of Erydia is incredibly powerful. "There's just so much to understand."

Asani is in his own world of observation.

He walks and tries to touch the feminine shadow, belonging to Latrice. But he's too slow. "I cannot touch it."

He asks himself, "Why not?"

Five, the strange evil being, is present as well. He has finished securing a strange rod from the young man. He then sees that something has Asani's attention. "Asani, what's the matter with you?"

Latrice heard that, and she says out loud, "Asani?" And then she quickly slaps her hand over her mouth.

Five hears it, but Asani does not.

And in that split instant, the Spirit Rhaija's voice is able to hone in on Latrice, "Why should you have to settle?"

The frustration of being ignored by Asani triggers the memory of how it used to be with Rick. The Spirit Rhaija then asks Latrice, "Why should it have to be this way? Why can't you just enjoy this moment?"

Latrice, remembering the words of Kaylandria, says, "No."

But this new Spirit senses something different, and knows that it's too late.

And no more voices speak. Latrice knew that she was not supposed to. But what was the harm in just saying that one word?

Five was just about to leave but he decides to stick around for a moment. "My boy, did I just hear someone call your name?"

Latrice shakes her head in regret.

Asani responds, "You know, I think I did."

Five slowly makes his way over to Asani and whispers in his ear. "Say something?"

Asani just looks at Five.

Latrice finds a huge rock to shield her shadow so that neither Five nor Asani can detect her. The sun is in a perfect position where it can cast no shadow.

Five loses the moment. "Say something, anything."

Asani turns his head a little and sees a fraction of an unclaimed shadow. "It's probably not a good idea."

Five says, "Nonsense."

"That was interesting. Maybe it will happen again."

Ch 44

And in that very moment, Latrice then finds herself in a special place of holding. The area and the colors are elongated, dominated by blurred greys, warm, very organic, as if they were alive.

Latrice utters, "Okay, where am I now?"

Kaylandria's voice calls out, "Don't you worry about where you are? I told you not to say anything, and what do you do?"

"Yeah, okay, I said something."

Kaylandria says, "Yeah, okay, you did say something. So now, okay, you have to go. Just forget about all of this."

"Wait. I didn't say I was ready to go?"

"I didn't ask you."

"Wait. Let's get one thing straight."

"Goodbye, Latrice."

And in that split second, Kaylandria sends Latrice away. She senses what's happening. Her body begins to dissipate.

Latrice says, "Wait. Wait. Who was the voice?"

There is a pause, but Kaylandria decides to say, "I'm sure you could tell that it wasn't me."

"Well who was she?"

"Rhaija. When you went against my wishes and spoke, you opened a door for her to enter and hear you. Now she knows that you are in the house."

Latrice responds, "What do you mean? Why didn't you tell me?"

"Because you didn't need to know."

"Well it would have helped to know the consequence to an action. You can't be just telling me half-handed information."

"I knew I couldn't count on you."

"What are you, betting on me to lose? Yeah, well, I want to go back and learn more."

And Latrice's body comes back into the strange holding place.

Kaylandria is so annoyed, she doesn't know what to do with herself. "For what? You are making a mess of things."

Latrice responds, "I mess of what? I heard Five mention that he has a rod."

Once again, that snags Kaylandria's ear. "You heard what? You did not hear that!"

Latrice adds, "Well, why not?"

"Well nevermind."

Kaylandria stops to ponder. Rhaija might have learned how to shield her thoughts from her.

Kaylandria allows some of herself to appear before Latrice. "Thank you. By you not listening to me, you allowed Rhaija to block my hearing."

Latrice responds, "What? How? I heard everything just fine."

"Yes, which has me wondering. I see. Could it be?"

Latrice is clueless, "What could what be?"

"Of course. You have a connection with Asani."

Latrice laughs, "Huh?"

Kaylandria says, "I am going to allow you to go back. I need you to observe. And I do mean observe."

Latrice asks, "Well what about the keys to the rooms?"

Kaylandria responds, "If you do what you are supposed to do, you will earn your keys."

CH 45

Kaylandria holds Latrice in a space that looks like a dark room where an abusive parent would place a child in timeout.

Latrice says, "So, what are you trying to show me now?"

"I have seen and felt so much cold heartedness, harm, strife, envy and hate from people across the span of this universe all of my life."

Latrice responds, "That's a long time. Sorry to hear that."

"At one point, I had to come into the House, to this room, and just let go."

"Let go of what?"

Kaylandria says, "Anything. People, thoughts, disappointments, anger, sadness... those things that were stolen that you gave up on trying to find."

And that makes Latrice sad, "Has there ever been any happiness in your life?"

Then very pretty medium sized wireframe shapes of amazing colors slowly float around Latrice.

Kaylandria says, "I come here to let go."

Latrice says, "Amazing. And then be free."

"All right, look. You were visible or your shadow was a vision in the sun the last time, and that was how Five was able to see you."

Latrice asks, "Why is Asani talking to that scrawny dwarf-like thing?"

Kaylandria refuses to say but her thoughts say to Latrice, "I cannot tell you."

"You cannot allow me to see him, and you cannot tell me the information I need. Why are you hating on me?"

"I promise you that it will all make sense. It is important to... hating on you? What does that mean? I hardly even know you!"

Latrice responds, "You act like that's my fault. We just met!"

Kaylandria takes a moment before she responds, "I am taking a huge risk in allowing you to go back, but it appears that I have no choice. Very well, take yourself back."

Latrice says, "Wait. Aren't you going to whisk me off with the wave of your hand or something?"

Kaylandria smiles, "No. You're going to learn to know where and when you belong."

Latrice stands a little confused. She cannot help but to think of the warmth that she feels when she's near Asani.

Kaylandria says, "Latrice..."

"I know. I know."

"You cannot be seen, and..."

"I know. Nor can I be heard. But how can I go there and not be seen. They're going to be looking for my shadow."

"Be creative. Remember what you have at your disposal, you're inside of a House that allows you to use your imagination while existing in reality."

"See that's the part I'm having trouble grasping."

Kaylandria interjects, "You're wasting time."

Latrice says, "Well excuse me. Bye."

And Kaylandria doesn't respond.

Latrice says, "Hello?"

Again, no response.

Latrice says, "Okay."

And in that instant, Latrice thinks about the last space where she saw Asani, and she leaves the Kaylandria's strange holding area. Latrice then materializes at the site of the rock where she concealed the shadow of her presence.

Kaylandria's voice quietly says, "Move quickly and do not linger in a space once you do not see what it is that you're looking for."

Latrice takes about two or three seconds to scout the area with her very clever shadow.

"You know that they are gone. How do you find out where they've gone?"

Latrice looks around. "I don't know."

"You have to clear your mind. Let this House of Erydia speak to you."

And in that split second, Latrice sees a glimpse of Asani facing a certain direction.

Kaylandria quietly says, "Feel his signature. Allow him to trace his steps for you."

Latrice quickly moves her body along the path where Asani and the strange being are moving.

Latrice feels a rush of confidence through this new power. Step by step, along the anticipated walking path of Asani and Five, Latrice closes the distance between them.

Kaylandria utters in a slightly louder voice, "Why are you moving so fast?"

Latrice ignores her and then says, "This is second nature."

"Slow down. Don't get in front of them."

"I can feel their steps."

Then Latrice sees Asani and Five. She's caught up to them.

Kaylandria yells, "Hey!"

Latrice stops in her tracks, and her body gets stuck inside the mass of rock that leads into a strange cave.

"I can't move." And she's right. She can hardly move her jaw. Her body is completely integrated with the cave. One physical form has joined another. But one of her feet is half way hanging out."

"Pull it together."

"But it hurts. I can't."

Kaylandria quietly responds, "Become."

Latrice responds, "Become what? I can hardly talk."

There is no response.

Latrice gasps to speak. "Become. Become. Become... the cave?"

And with that thought, even though she was not 100% sure, Latrice's body takes on a new form, allowing her to be all that the cave is. Her body embraces its form, the arced passage way, even the mildew, and Latrice cannot believe it.

Five and Asani come before the entrance to the cave which is now being consumed by Latrice's altered state.

CH 46

Five gets to thinking. "Hmm... I should have... It doesn't matter."

Asani is steadily trying to follow. "What's wrong?"

Five waves it off. "Ah, nothing. Don't worry about it. Okay. It's just that I should have had you bring two more rods instead of just one."

Asani stands with a peculiar look. "How?"

Five walks up to Asani. "Well when you come back with another rod. I can show you. You'll be able to think of any place and blink, and you will be there in an instant."

Latrice hears this and thinks to herself. "That sounds familiar."

There are no words, no sounds that can escape her. She not only hears but feels the intention of every word, every action. But she knows better to act on anything, and to say nothing.

Asani responds, "How can that be?"

Five begins to walk down a path within the cave. "Oh don't worry about it. What is the use if I cannot show you?" And he stops walking and something jolts Asani.

"So you knew my father?" Asani asks.

And Five smirks, "Oh yes. Your father. You, Asani, come from a very impressive group of people. Unfortunately, they would become enslaved for over four centuries. And that the same measure of injustice that was shown to your ancestors, some might say was their own fault. To be truly free, one must face a great awakening in order to be fully cleansed and reconciled."

Five continues, "Your father, King Antonias, had ways about himself that were so very foreign to his people at the time. He was radical, forward in his thinking, some may say a little too forward. His big ideas frightened his people. While his vision for a better way of life would have made his kingdom better off, those very same people were very resistant to change, and thinking on their own. Everyone needed to feel relevant, almost like a plague of insecurity. King Antonias wanted to liberate his people through thinking on their own, but the powers that be, which was the newly formed Senate, did not approve.

Latrice listens on and is thinking to herself, "How does he know this?"

Five continues explaining to the young man, "Your father's vision... was left incomplete. You were revived to do that which was not finished."

Asani asks, "How do you know this?"

That made Latrice smile and say to herself, "Exactly."

"Asani, your father stood before the Senate and pleaded, 'What is so terribly wrong about being on our own? Why must we remain dependent when we do not have to? Sure, it will not be as great as what we have now. But the difference is, it will be ours. It will belong to us and us alone.'"

And Asani asks Five, "Why wouldn't they listen?"

Five responds, "Because there was no room for compromise. Your father, Antonias, was considered by some to be closed minded. But we live and we learn."

"Feel the words. Don't just hear them." Kaylandria's voice says to Latrice.

Latrice, still in her current morphed state, says, "Something's wrong."

Latrice sees something strange. Her mind opens up and begins to see Five trying to convince this council to transfer power over from the Senate. For the King, who has no face, has passed. Antonias is mourning. But the council respected the wishes of this King. And Latrice is even further enlightened. She goes back to listening to the words uttered inside of her cave.

Five continues speaking to Asani, "Both of your parents were assassinated. But your mother sent you, the only son, away into hiding."

Asani is gripped with confusion. "Though I never knew my mother…"

Five looks on and touches Asani on his arm with his little hand. "Every child should have an opportunity to see, feel, and to touch their parents."

The information that Five is saying is so rich. Asani and Latrice are hanging onto every word.

Five adds, "But that's enough."

Asani had been all alone up until now. He was beginning to feel comforted by the words of this miniature person. "Was there anyone else who is here now with you then?"

And Five bends back with a rich bellowing laugh. "What's the matter? You don't believe me? No my lad, unfortunately all you have to go on is what I remember from years and years ago."

Five and Asani reach the end of the cave.

Asani hands Five the rods.

Five walks ahead of Asani, going through a porthole. "Ah, ah, ah, only I am permitted."

Asani asks, "Where does it lead?"

"I'm sorry, but that is only for me to know. You wouldn't understand even if I told you."

Five reaches up and grabs Asani by the back of his neck and pulls him down on a face to face level. "You run along and get me the next rod. I want to tell you more."

Asani understands, "When will you return?"

"Soon."

And Five walks off into the strange blinding powerful yellow light.

It was so powerful that it made Latrice gasp for air, as if something had left her womb all of a sudden. The very familiar feeling makes Latrice lose her concentration. Latrice tries to hold on to her stealth form, but she finally comes out of it, falling to the dry cold sand. After she gets the sand out of her mouth, she realizes that she could be seen by Asani. But he was already on his way out, and by now leaving the cave all together.

Latrice realizes that she can now see and touch herself. She wonders how. She looks at the porthole and then looks back in the other direction.

She walks out of the cave and then she amazingly resumes her shape through shadows. Under this guise, she gladly follows Asani to wherever he's going. He's out of sight but he's left a trace of steps in the sand. Invisible ponytail swinging and all, Latrice decides to pick up her pace to make sure she doesn't lose him.

"What are you doing?" Kaylandria's voice asks.

Latrice stops and looks up above and then off to the side. She quickly realizes who it is. "I have information. And now I need some more."

"For what? Where are you are going now?"

Latrice says nothing as she jogs on to her destination.

"I would really advise you against it. I wish that you wouldn't."

Latrice responds, "I'm not saying anything to him."

Kaylandria appears but says nothing. She takes a moment to sit on a rock, and starts overlooking some of the beautiful strange terrain.

Latrice stops and turns around. "What? No parting instructions?"

"No. You'll discover what you need as you go."

Latrice responds, "I don't know what I'm looking for, but I'm having a good time doing it."

Kaylandria says nothing. Latrice walks away and then she smirks a little.

CH 47

Just a little while later in the living room of the strange isolated western style ranch house, Bowers is confronting Asani, "That's not true. I'm the one that knew your father! And to be honest, sometimes I could not stand him."

That gets Asani's attention.

Bowers adds, "Antonias... Antonias... always something special... something nice being said about Antonias."

The stealthy Latrice has followed Asani back to the strange house. The land, the soil, the lay of the land is just not anything that she's ever seen. She arrives and comes up the steps where she finds him and Bowers in a heated discussion. She thinks to herself, "Where on earth am I?"

She ponders what the concept for time is. She feels as if there is not enough, or is that just her feeling cast aside once more? What Latrice did not realize was that she was light years away from the Earth.

Bowers continues to reflect with Asani listening, "I was a servant of the King's family, and personal playmate to your father Antonias. We grew up together. Like his father, your father excelled in science, astronomy in particular. I would eventually become your father's assistant because I knew just as much, and in some cases more, than Antonias. Early on, we were very competitive but eventually we called each other friend. And I do not take that for granted. For it did not have to be that way. Why tamper with the very fiber of memories that held you in dominant power over another when you do not have to? My family started out as servants. But when Antonias became king, I became his friend. Right before the Second Departure, I swore an oath to look after you as if you were my very own."

Bowers remembers the moment that baby Asani was placed in the stasis chamber. "Your father disappeared first. Your mother gave their only son to me to look after. Your grandfather was the true leader.

If you had to categorize his reign, he would have been called "The King of the First Departure."

There's a gentle breeze that caresses the low quality sage green drapes, allowing for a better view into the house. Latrice has heard bits and pieces from Bowers. She remembers while chatting with Asani online, Latrice actually caught glimpses of Bowers, but never before has she seen him like this. He seems extremely bothered.

Latrice quickly assesses that the only way into the house without being noticed is through the front window, which is to the right of the front door.

It looks as if the window is being very discreetly pushed up. Bowers is at the table in the kitchen nervously twitching his left leg. But he sees the window going up, then down a little.

Bowers is beyond caring about looking crazy. He says, "Who's that?"

Latrice knows that her actions have been noticed, but she's somewhat confident that her stealth will keep her protected. She comes all the way into the house and to her shocking surprise her stealth ability wears off. And Bower's neurotic eyes quickly fall onto this intruder.

Impulsively, Bowers grabs a nearby kitchen knife and runs towards Latrice.

Latrice is so wide-eyed and shocked that this wild crazy looking man is coming at her full speed that she cannot find any words to say but "Help!"

And Bowers is certainly not bothering to ask any questions.

Bowers raises a brand new extremely sharp knife in his left hand, and Asani yells, "No!"

Too late, it's coming down in a hurry as she shuns her face. But Bowers misses somehow.

Latrice yells. "Asani!"

Bowers is off balance and falls to the floor.

He gets up. Asani says, "Wait, don't! Latrice?"

Bowers looks a little harder and then back at Asani. "The computer girl? How did you get here?"

She says nothing.

Bowers says, "If you don't tell me right now who you really are, you are going to be in a world of trouble."

Bowers tries to grab her arm and he grabs nothing but air. He looks at her, looks at his hand, and tries it again.

Same thing happens. "How did you do that?

Latrice looks just as dumbfound.

Both of them are on the floor getting splinters from the hard wood and Bowers asks, "Why can't I touch you?"

Latrice breathes a huge sigh of relief, "I don't know, but I sure am glad that you can't."

Asani comes from the next room where he was observing. He walks into the living room in complete silence. "Is that you?"

Still a little scared, Latrice responds, "Yeah, I guess."

Asani cannot believe his eyes. He slowly comes over to Latrice. He wants to help her up, but he knows that that's not possible. Finally, she stands up to lock eyes with the long awaited object of her attention. "Are you happy that I am here?"

Bowers says, "That ain't her!"

Asani responds, "Well, why not?"

Bowers goes silent, "It's just not. Trust me."

Latrice says, "It is!"

Bowers responds, "Don't make me… you know what… we'll just see."

He scurries out of the room.

Latrice says, "Where's he going?"

Ch 48

Upstairs, what is probably the attic of the home, Asani pushes the large door like windows open and they sit on the edge. There is an interesting beautiful night sky full of miraculous stars.

Latrice says, "Wow. Oh my goodness. I have never seen a sky like this before."

"Well, it is just that..." He's caught up looking at Latrice's beautiful profile.

She turns to him. "What?"

He turns away.

"So you're the girl that I've been talking to?"

Latrice responds, "In the flesh... well... not exactly, but I am here... at least the part that matters."

Asani's body jerks around nervously in excitement, "So what you're telling me is that you're actually not here, but in a home somewhere else."

"Precisely."

"Should I be trusting you?"

Latrice responds, "You should do whatever your heart tells you to do."

Asani tries to touch her hand, but he feels nothing. His effort made Latrice feel wonderful.

"Then why am I not able to touch you?"

Latrice responds, "Well, how come I'm not able to touch you? Who's to say that you're not real?"

Asani goes around and knocks on the end table. Then he rubs his strong hand on the upper part of the sofa cushion, never taking his eyes off of Latrice. She gets a little embarrassed.

Asani says, "You ever feel like you exist, but you don't know how?"

Latrice drags her beautiful eyes around Asani's wonderful face. "Now I do."

Asani continues, "I've been told so much today that I don't really know what's real and what's not.

"How so?"

"Kings, kingdoms... like I told you on... line... I'm just trying to figure me out."

And then there's nothing said.

Asani tries to get closer to her. It is obvious, he's getting turned on. She naturally looks down and sees that he's got that nice fat hard-on for her once more.

"Hey, I know you?"

He goes to touch Latrice, and his hand touches nothing. That's what she gets for objectifying his little leg of blood flow.

Latrice herself is so turned on, she does not know what to do. He tries to touch her again... same thing.

Her breathing gets more extreme. "What's wrong? How come we can't touch each other?"

Asani responds, "I don't know."

He tries again and again, but the restriction, the frustration, and now the close distance are enough drive any woman absolutely mad.

Latrice says, "Are you sure?"

A gasping Asani responds, "Yes."

"Because I really like being touched."

"Well, I don't know what to do."

Latrice then removes her short sleeve button down and places it on the side. Asani's eyes slowly become a little wider.

Latrice says, "Do you mind?"

Asani has absolutely no idea of what he's agreeing to but he says, "Yes. I mean no."

That was just the go-ahead-signal that Latrice was looking for to remove her grey t-shirt. She starts fondling herself, caressing your breasts, and then she begins to unzip her pants. "I need to touch her."

Asani responds, "She, who?"

"Her."

"Yeah?"

"Yes."

"Are you gonna pull him out?"

"Am I gonna do what?"

Latrice says nothing.

Asani looks at the door, "Wait."

"No."

"I just wanna lock the door."

"Just pull it out."

"Pull what out?"

She goes to try to touch his it, but she can't. "Oh just pull it out."

And he slowly undoes the drawstring to his strange olive green pants.

Latrice turns around and gets herself situated, cocking her leg open, and starts moaning as she touches herself. "Did you know that you turn me on? Hm? Did you know that?"

Asani just gazes helplessly upon the first naked woman that he has ever seen and releases, "Yes."

"I can't take your bottoms off. You're gonna do that for me?"

"Okay."

She's licking the tip of her middle and ring finger and then places them down in her favorite place of choice. "Mmm. I wish we could make love."

"Make love? What do you mean?"

"You're joking right?"

"No."

"Oh, if we could touch each other, I could show you."

Asani looks a little afraid. Latrice notices. "I would make you feel so good honey."

Asani is just as shy as he could be as his ears take in Latrice's wonderful sighing. He begins to take his pants off and she sees the huge muscles in his thighs. "Oh good lord, just look at you. Goodness. Are you kidding? Oh baby come here and kiss me."

Just as Asani is removing his black undergarment, he disappears. Latrice utters, "What the…?"

The room is empty with just Latrice. She looks around and then over her shoulder. "Where did he go?"

And in comes Kaylandria, "What do you call yourself doing? Put your clothes on, right now.

"Excuse me, you are not my mother."

"I mean it, right now."

"I am so serious!"

"If you do not want our time together to end, you should listen to me."

"Girl if you don't go somewhere and come back later!"

Kaylandria calmly says, "You need to pull yourself together."

"How bout, no, you bring Asani back." Latrice is so annoyed as she realizes that her moment is departing fast.

Latrice is just about ready to throw a tantrum, "You did that. You bring him back here, right now."

"No."

Latrice puts her shirt on. Kaylandria just shakes her head. "Why must the female species always get so fixated on men?"

Latrice responds, "What? What do you mean fixated?"

Kaylandria says, "In the wake of his understanding, can't you see that he is confused?"

Meanwhile, Asani is still in the room, but he cannot see Latrice at all. He is looking rather desperatley around the old dusty furniture for her.

But Kaylandria has shielded them from each other's sight. Kaylandria could see both of them walking around the dusty attic space. Asani is looking behind all of the furniture that's all arrested to the walls.

"And so let me guess, it is up to me to help him find his way."

Kaylandria adds, "This is why you are here, in the House of Erydia. This is why you were chosen."

Latrice says, "Where or who is this Erydia?"

"Erydia is the place designated for all that should be, could be, and would be understood... another place that requires and grants freedom in thought. There will be a time for taking. But for now, you are here to observe and learn."

Oh that just burns Latrice up. She's still very much turned on. "Kaylandria, I need to teach you how to multi-task."

Kaylandria says, "I can tell that you're going to insist on doing this your way. I do not do this too often and I am not trying to apologize for what I am about to say, but I would like to remind you of your history with your previous love."

Latrice looks at her. "Excuse me?"

"I think you really should have seen Rick, all alone."

"I think you need to shut your mouth."

"All he needed was for someone to just look into his eyes for just a moment. The soft caress of a hand could have wiped away at least some of his despair and given comfort to the very essence of his soul.

"You got a thing for my husband, don't you?"

Kaylandria walks over to the window and stares out at a moon, lost in a thought of her own, "In that moment, Rick would have been reminded that you were the most important, the only person who truly mattered to him. But instead, you chose to abandon him."

Latrice lashes out, "So is this all that you do, invade people's space? What was I supposed to do, just let him have his way in everything? What about me? I have a life too. When will I matter? Why are his needs so much greater than mine?"

Kaylandria has her back turned to Latrice so that her unhappy facial expressions can remain concealed. This way she can take in every word spoken. "I do understand how you feel, but in this particular instance, this is how it is. And this is how it will be. I am trying to protect the both of you."

Latrice asks, "Are you trying to keep me away from Asani?"

Kaylandria says, "I do not know what you are speaking of."

"Of course you don't . Let's be real. What do you really want?"

"Have you asked yourself why you're able to be seen here in the house and not outside?"

With ease and haste, Kaylandria clutches Latrice's hand and sticks it outside. "You see? I have enabled you to have some aspects of your physical appearance here."

Latrice responds, "I was gonna ask you about that."

"I am fine with you speaking with Asani here. But you cannot do that beyond the perimeter of this house."

Latrice says, "Why? What makes him so special?"

"You need me to answer that for you?

Latrice just stands still with arms folded, tapping her index finger on her forearm.

"There are those who have been on a quest for Asani for many of your Earth's ages. Rhaija is one of those individuals. Well, she is more of a spirit entity than anything else."

Arms still folded, and now beginning to pace the floor with long slowful strides, "I'm a little confused."

"Originally after the inception of the Earth, the Sprit Rhaija was an entity composed of soft purposeful energy. She was present whenever she sensed a group of people all on one accord who were ready to take a leap of faith away from the Earth. She was and still is very calculating, all knowing on most levels, and some believe she is all present. That is to say, that you cannot make a sound, whisper, blink an eye, or have a thought that could escape her senses."

Latrice says, "You're making her sound like some sort of goddess or something."

"Some might say she is a little lower than a god. She's tangible to some, but illusive, charming, and cunning to most."

The Spirit presented itself, oh I'm sorry, excuse me, herself to Asani's grandfather, King Gakuru.

"Wait, King? And which country is this again? I get that we're in the past. I'm confused. I don't think Asani, that other crazy dude. What's his name?"

Kaylandria says, "Bowers."

"Yeah, him. And me... none of us know where we are."

There's a second of awkward silence.

Kaylandria says, "What?"

"What do you mean 'what'? Where am I?"

"With me, of course. In the House of..."

"Erydia... right." Latrice can feel herself getting frustrated, but she lets it go. She refuses to give in to a feeling of craziness that wants to latch itself. So she starts to laugh it off.

"It's not funny. As I was saying, King Gakuru was amazed and in awe by this surprise visit from above. She was very complimentary of the way he served his people. She offered him an opportunity to serve his people in an entirely different way. The Spirit Rhaija showed Asani's grandfather a way of life that would change the course of his time. She offered him a means by which to stay close to her, and learn more proficient and compassionate ways of loving his people. Rhaija's beauty was indeed something to behold. She stood almost twice as tall as Asani's grandfather. And her presence was arresting. A human could only see her for moments at a time. For her beauty would render the strongest mortal helpless."

Latrice asks, "Why does this affect Asani now and let's say his ability to interact with someone like me?"

Kaylandria shakes her head and thinks, "Really Latrice?"

"What? Why can't you tell me."

"Because I do not trust you."

Latrice is taken aback, "What do you mean? Who are you not to be trusting anyone, the one who comes and goes as she pleases?"

Kaylandria interjects, "I asked you not to speak to Asani while in your Shadow, and what do you do? You come up here and get naked?"

Latrice knows that she's wrong but she still says, "We ain't do nothin'."

"I know. And you have me to thank for that."

Latrice throws up her hands, "You know, this is too…"

Kaylandria cuts over her, "Fine, leave… now."

Latrice takes a moment to compose herself. "How much of this information does Asani know? Who is explaining this to him?"

"If I had to take a guess, I'd say Bowers. But his memory has been affected by Five, who must be stopped. Bowers is Asani's protector and the guardian of the Rods of the Yeswe'."

"Rods of the Ya'hoo?"

"Yeswe'."

"Now what is that?"

"In good time… you will get an explanation."

"Kaylandria."

"I promise, soon, but I have to go."

"What are these rods?"

Kaylandria says, "There are five."

"Wait. Does Asani know what you just told me?"

"Probably not."

"Why not? You are killing me with what he knows and what he doesn't. How is he going to know?"

Kaylandria comes closer to Latrice and within inches of her face says, "I want you to figure that out."

"How?"

"By learning when and when not to speak."

"Excuse me?"

She grabs Latrice by the sides of her beautiful face and kisses her forehead.

Kaylandria takes a step through the window and walks out onto thin air, and walks away. And she turns around, "And one more thing."

Latrice pouts a little as she stands on the edge of the opening. "What Kaylandria?"

"Do not tell him nor Bowers of your mission."

"What mission? I don't know my mission."

"Your mission is to learn and observe. And you are doing a subpar job at best."

"Who's going to tell Asani what he needs to know?"

Kaylandria touches Latrice's hand, "Appearances can be deceiving."

It has been just a little while since the ladies have left the strange ranch house. With the wave of her hand, Kaylandria shows Latrice glimpses of Bowers in that house, struggling to overcome Five's spell. He is wrapped up in a thick warm grey blanket, huddled on the floor in the corner of the dark damp kitchen. "Asani is already in excellent hands."

That comforts Latrice.

"Wait! Where are you going?"

"You will see. In a little while, walk outside and stand under the cloud which finds its way over the house. That will be your cue to leave. Do not tarry."

Kaylandria takes a couple more steps on her path of air, and then flies off as if she was a bird, one never before seen by Latrice. She marvels at its sheer beauty.

The moment thaws. Asani and Latrice miraculously appear in each other's space once again.

Asani is about to pull down his drawers, only to discover that he has no drawers. Latrice tries to stop him, but her hand goes through his body by accident.

"No. No. No. Don't."

"What's wrong? I thought that you disappeared because I didn't show you…"

Latrice responds, "Just pull em' up. Ooo wait. No, pull em' up!"

Asani redoes his draw string, allowing the fabric to breathe and stretch over his beautiful body once again.

CH 49

Just as Kaylandria instructed, Latrice begins to find her way outside. Asani walks her down the pitch black staircase to the front door.

"You're such a gentleman. Someone raised you right."

Asani leans up against the wall with his hands in his pocket, and then scratching the back of his head.

Latrice says, "So I have a question. Where are we?"

Asani replies, "What?"

"I mean I think I know, but I don't know."

"What difference does it make?" Asani replies.

"Never mind, I just want you to come visit me."

While Asani and Latrice are talking, Bowers walks by eating a bowl of hot leftovers, with his itchy but warm blanket underneath his arm. He backs up... and shakes his head at their shenanigans and continues on.

Latrice says to Asani, "Whatever you're doing, he seems to be getting better, I hope."

Asani replies, "Well, if he has another setback, I'll protect you."

"Like last time? No thank you."

Asani replies, "Will I be able to touch you if I come see you."

Latrice smiles. "That would make me happy."

But in this moment, there is no touching. They do not even try. Even though they absolutely wish that they could. They settle for the satisfaction of what their unfiltered senses of sight will allow.

Asani opens the door, and Latrice waves goodbye to him. As soon as she crosses the wood threshold, Latrice then returns to the form of her

Shadow. She knows better than to say anything to Asani at this point.

But while scraping his blue bowl for that last good spoonful, Bowers goes over to the front room window and watches Latrice along with Asani, who now steps out on the porch. They both watch Latrice's form find her way through the soft sand mix in the front yard. And then the Shadow of Latrice disappears.

Asani's eyes are still able to follow Latrice ascending to the largest cloud over his strange enigmatic house. Bowers was certainly glad to see Latrice leave, for he was afraid that the truth would be exposed. For Asani and Bowers were both living on a strange uninhabited world, one made just for the two of them, in a sector of uncharted space in order to remain hidden from their enemies.

That made Bowers reflect back on his parents leaving him. They died in an exploration accident in a treacherous mountain range (somewhere near the Himalayas). He remembers praying and hoping for a safe return, but word got back to the Kingdom that Mera and Remi had died from an avalanche. It was Asani's father who learned that they had a son and that he needed to be told. This son had been hoping and praying for his parents' safe return. The need to be connected to his parents created a hunger to believe in something… someone. And Bowers had a closer relationship with his mother, like most boys, and appealed to the heavens to place his care in the loving hands of a female spirit. It was a quiet but zealous bitter prayer.

As Bowers matured, he became fascinated with doors, portholes, and pathways. It was said by Juria, a very attractive woman friend, that Bowers was searching for something. But even he did not know what he sought. One thing for sure was that he rejected the first encounter with the Creator, but rather sought the comfort of a god with a female persona. Eventually, Bowers found her, or rather he and Rhaija found each other. And she was beautiful, but not just in her outer appearance, but she seemed to say all the things that Bowers needed to hear. For his heart was sincerely broken over the loss of his parents.

Bowers had produced the hope of 1000 Faithful Warriors. It was strong, raw, and most of all misdirected. Bowers didn't feel at liberty to have the right to believe in what his heart was connected to.

So for Bowers to now see Asani connecting so naturally with Latrice was more than his newly awakened heart could bear. For even through a four and a half billion year slumber, Mera and Remi were still so very close, so very present in Bowers' thoughts.

Back in front of the strange ranch style house, Latrice was several thousand feet into the air and she begins to feel something strange on her body which allows her to be lighter than air itself. She says to herself, "Maybe I just should just go home."

Kaylandria's voice says, "And miss what has been prepared for you? You've barely begun."

Asani comes even further out into the yard and just stares at her, as she turns her head back and sighs at what she's leaving behind.

"Don't worry. He will be fine."

"You promise?"

"I cannot make any guarantees but that is the hope."

Cн 50

In this incredible set of terrific but strange slightly overcast clouds, Latrice finds herself tumbling into what resembles a hallway, or a set of circular corridors whose walls are as puffy as the outer clouds themselves.

Kaylandria's voice starts from afar and bounces its echo off the inner walls of these strange clouds, and finally arriving to Latrice. "Follow the path of the soft lights."

The words are so peaceful and delightful as each syllable caresses Latrice's sensitive and stressed inner ear.

Kaylandria says, "Let go. Your true happiness awaits."

But Latrice cannot help but to think of Asani. She admits to herself aloud, "He makes me happy."

"I know, but forget about him for now. Everyone has thoughts, feelings, visions, and dreams. These Clouds of Escah are wonders that allow you to rid yourself of old and painful memories."

Latrice just shakes her head and sighs. "You just will not give up, will you?"

"If we take a trip into your own thoughts, specifically those with Rick, I can help you to release them, if you wish."

"It really isn't anything to see."

"Thank you."

The first distinctive voice signature is heard. Latrice knows to head to the right. But she has to watch her footing because the floor is cloud-soft.

"I feel like a lab rat."

"Move quickly. Throw your body in my direction... arms out. Now!"

And she does. The wind outside of the clouds blows rather fiercely and hurls Latrice back in the opposite direction. "It's too hard for me to control!"

"Concentrate."

"I am!"

"Where and how did you and Rick meet?"

"What?"

"Answer the question?"

Latrice sees that the direction that she's falling back towards will soon dump her out on the other end of the strange cloud.

Kaylandria's voice says, "You're not concentrating."

Latrice's body is halfway outside the comfort and security of the cloud. "I don't believe you!"

"And then if you fall, please believe that you will indeed fall."

"I met him at Howard!"

The other end of the cloud immediately closes up, and Latrice falls to the soft floor of the cloud. But she starts sinking and soon sees a distressful view of the ground far below. Kaylandria says, "Get up."

And Latrice gets up and awkwardly jumps into the air once more. She's starting to fatigue. She gets control over her body again and moves forward.

Kaylandria says, "Please continue."

And in that moment, Latrice sighs and allows her mind to connect to Kaylandria's question, drifting back to a moment neatly tucked away. These are the moments that Kaylandria has been waiting an eternity to discover:

Latrice transferred to Howard University in 1997. When she first came onto the yard, there was a mix up in the rooms in the female dorm. And she ended up having to stay off campus with a slightly older woman, Shonnie. Living next door to Shonnie was Rickland Foster.

It was a humid August Tuesday right before school started and they bumped into each other in the hallway of their DC apartment building. Rick had just finished his PT coming in drenched at 7am. And Latrice was just leaving the apartment where she was renting a room from Shonnie. She was by the window stretching, bending over and Rick was coming off the elevator and her ass was just perfect.

Rick thought that he had walked right into his destiny. He had a hard time saying anything at first but then after a month of seeing Latrice in his passing, he finally worked up a nerve to try to hold a meaningful conversation. But by then, it was a little too late.

One night, one of the US Senators from Florida, Ron Jacobs, invited Rick to the Senate Committee fundraiser on Space and Sciences. "Either make time... or waste time."

Both Rick and Latrice were invited. Latrice was fond of Ron's work and contributions to the advancement of keeping space exploration limited to fact based theories and assumptions. Where Rick was much more interested in something more free and spirit based. Senator Jacobs would sometimes be brave enough to say, "Boy you ain't nothin' but a lil space hippie ain't you?"

President Clinton had called Senator Jacobs and he had to leave the party. He asked Rick, who was decked out in his service uniform, "Would you make sure that my Town Car gets Latrice home safely?"

It doesn't line up any better than that. Rick wasn't necessarily the most polished, but at least he was the perfect gentleman. Latrice was looking extra fine in that Christian Dior dress... back exposed... four inch stilettoes... hair pinned up... exposing her beautiful neck. She moved so gracefully. Senator Jacobs leaves instructions, but Latrice says, "I'm grown. I don't live on campus. I don't have a curfew." And Rick smiles. They walk outside and lo and behold, what does Rick see? "Excuse me is this limo by any chance reserved for Senator Jacobs?"

Latrice comes to an abrupt stop in the cloud. "Wait."

Kaylandria says, "I would suggest that you keep moving forward. That is if you do not want to sink through the floor."

Latrice finds herself once more starting to slowly sink through the floor of the clouds below. "Look, if you pulled me up here to probe me and get me to talk about him…"

Kaylandria responds, "I highly suggest you keep moving forward."

"I see where this is going, I keep from dying as long as I play this little game."

"Exactly."

"Why is any of this important to you?"

"You can say that the Creator has given you an opportunity to rid yourself of all of this heaviness that you've been carrying."

And Latrice says, "And everything that I reveal will be left here in the cloud?"

"Naturally. That was my idea from the very start."

Latrice sighs. "Okay. What else do you wish to know?"

"Thank you for asking."

"How were you with money?"

Latrice responds, "What?"

And so her motion of flight within the strange clouds begins to slow. "All right, all right, fine, since you want to invade my thoughts!"

"I am not invading your thoughts. You came into the house on your own free will. The experience in the House is symbolic of you, your past, your present..."

Latrice responds, "And what? My future?"

"I will entertain this question. Your future, your past, and your present in this space are all one."

That's a satisfactory response for Latrice, "That doesn't make sense."

"And yet you're curious enough to move forward. How were you and Rick with money?"

Latrice mumbles, "How were we with money?" She allows her mind to drift.

Money has never been a problem, nor an issue. Latrice and Rick were both good with money. However, Rick was more generous. Latrice would call it being frivolous. Rick has always believed that tomorrow would truly take care of itself.

Kaylandria, who was apparently remotely situated, then asks, "So what happened to cause you two to separate?"

It's not like Latrice had to do any work in verbally expressing these answers. Her mind did all of the talking.

A few years into their relationship, non-profit organizations would target their household to give. Rick and Latrice would get into arguments and she would say, "You can't think you can just save the world. You're one person. You're spending my money, and this is really getting on my nerves."

And that would set Rick's teeth on edge. "Well it's my money too and if I want to give to good causes I should be able to do so."

Latrice says to Kaylandria, "My money, his money, money ate at our relationship more than anything."

So she would try to accept the strange way in which Rick would shut things down when things didn't go his way, and over the short term it would be okay. But Rick in turn does not see how it would affect her, "You just can't pretend that I'm not doing what I'm doing."

Rick shakes his head. "Listen, most of it's your money. So just do what you're doing and I'll be fine. I'll do what I want."

And that would make Latrice sad, "Well what kind of crappy relationship would that be?"

But as soon as they would get deep into an argument, Rick or Latrice would say something to make them remember why they fell in love.

Kaylandria says to Latrice, "So money was the problem, or was there something else?

Latrice's eyes would begin to gloss over with a thin layer from her tear. We'd try to make love to hopefully put an end to the quarreling."

But their tragedy was just great to ignore or mask with mere money.

Latrice recalls Rick saying, "You just had to go to that stupid ass fertility specialist that I told you not to go to. And look what happened."

"I didn't mean for that to happen. I just wanted to... I don't know. I wasn't thinking. It was like something heavy come over me. The specialist was so convincing. Rick didn't know. I didn't know. We just wanted to have our baby. But the more and more I think, we didn't deserve a child. I mean, why raise a child around all of our madness?"

Kaylandria is in a separate room, very dark, with her eyes closed, as she receives confirmation. "Rhaija."

Poor Latrice was now open and vulnerable once again to the hurt that she experiences. "Make it stop."

She could not help but to think back. Though Rick was not entirely wrong, his neglect, hurt, depression, and unforgiveness that followed affected him in such a way that it drove a wedge between he and Latrice. "Honey, please talk to me. Don't shut me out."

But that was Rick's biggest weakness, being able to expose his feelings. And because of that single occurrence of unforgiveness that day, the entire universe was affected and would never be the same.

Rick became selfish, and it wasn't too long before Latrice did the same. She had always dreamed of being the perfect little DC wife, but she put that on ice because Rick said to her one day, "Uh, I'm a scientist, not a Senator."

It would make Latrice sad because before they were married, he would hold her in his arms and tell her, "You're a dream come true, but ain't no way in the world I'm living near Clarence Thomas."

For Latrice, it was all about perception, and living a life of validation that stemmed from the appearance of power, one level on top of another, and that hunger would never be fulfilled.

And for a while after they married, Rick wanted to be the politically correct husband and do all of those right things that got him further into the know. But he could only fake it for so long. Rick found himself supporting causes that did not resonate with any of his core beliefs, all because they were spearheaded by individuals that were full of themselves.

But all of these issues and new found ways of redirecting their focus were just a cover-up. They wanted to be parents. Rick wanted to be a father and Latrice wanted to be a mother.

A familiar voice utters softly into Latrice's thoughts, "You might have impaired your husband's dream because of your own fears of being replaced and forgotten."

Latrice continues recounting what Rick said, "Look, what you are doing is affecting our livelihood."

And Rick would challenge her on it. "No... no... you mean your livelihood. I don't compromise my beliefs for anyone."

And Latrice challenges him, "That goes for me too!"

Rick takes a second to let her words fall on him. "Yes, it does."

But Latrice could read his face and his body language. She was very much in tune with Rick's feelings. But they both were guilty of arresting the truth. And now it needed to be set free.

The realities began to weigh too much on Rick's shoulders. Eventually, he knew what he needed to do. And it saddened him. He knew that she was slowly but surely choosing perception over true love. And for that, he knew that there would be no way to ever leave Latrice and not break his own heart. How would... how could he make it okay for him to leave? For his tolerance for Latrice and her schmoozing and kissing ass with this person, that person, this politician, and that interest group, it all just turned Rick away from what used to be so pure. Rick would have to realize and accept that Latrice had chosen to evolve... into someone else.

Rick would embark on a journey of estrangement after he had allowed the sad weight of the reality to set in on him, that the woman who he fell in love with, that moment in time was over, never to return.

Within this portion of the cloud, Kaylandria summarizes to Latrice. "On Spiritual record, whether you choose to accept this or not, Rick sent up one of the most fervent, passionate, soul stirring prayers, that when he cried out, it rattled the highest parts of the heavens."

Latrice asks, "I just want to know when will this be over?" It tore her apart to have to relive this.

"Patience. You will never have more than you can handle."

"Why are you doing this to me?"

Kaylandria responds, "I need for you to endure this journey into your past. Will you continue?"

The journey through the inner clouds of Escah continue. Latrice gives in. "Yes."

CH 51

Latrice was to receive an award for *Outstanding Fundraiser of the Year*. She's on the phone with Rick while she is in route to the restaurant. "I cooked some turkey tacos before I left."

Rick says, "Well, I thought you were gonna wait on me so we could go together."

"I didn't think you wanted to go."

"Well why not?"

"Well, because… you were the one who said that you didn't like being around those kind of people, remember?"

Rickland responds, "Listen all those people really don't mean anything. When it comes to you, I am here to support you in what you do. This is huge."

"Well I'll tell you about it when I come home."

"You still could have told me."

Latrice feels his tension. "I know, but they're being really tight on these invites."

The valet opens Latrice's car door. "Okay. Gotta go babe."

Rick just gets home himself. After he sets his shoulder bag down, he looks in the refrigerator and sees the plastic container with the taco meat. Before he goes any further, he sets the pen down on the table that he's had in his hand since he left work. He takes the plastic blue lid off the small large container and smells it. His facial expression is one of disapproval.

Rick has a thing about eating on nice plates. So he goes and grabs one out of the china cabinet. "So what if Latrice hates it. I paid for these plates too."

As Rick is picks through his less than satisfactory meal, his eyes so happen to fall on the other invite to the event on the end table.

Meanwhile, in a nice sized private room at *Oya* in DC, Senator Ron Jacobs is on the stage. "It is hard to find dedicated people who understand your vision. And that vision... it can still be carried out a number of different ways. But there is not just one way, one right way. That way is Latrice Foster's way. Latrice has been the brains and engine behind an operation that started out with little to no support. It certainly did not have backing. People who mindlessly throw hope and money behind a deteriorating space program are now looking at other options. Ladies and Gentlemen, please help me recognize and congratulate Ms. Latrice... Ms.? Ms. Latrice Williams."

Latrice gives him a look and he corrects himself, "Latrice Foster... Foster ladies and gentlemen."

Ron is just in his element. All of the right people are assembled, and he's feeling himself as he steps back from the podium in his new grey Brook's Brothers suit. He gestures for Latrice to come up. And she's looking ever so classy and ready to shine.

Just as she comes on stage, Rick has slipped inside undetected. He lays low and just stays in the cut.

Latrice comes to the podium and stands before a group of very well connected, politically savvy, and powerful people. She looks at Ron. Then she taps the inner part of her beautiful new wedding ring on the side of the lectern. It makes her feel comfortable before speaking. "Fighting world hunger and issues of health have to become more important. And I realize that when Senator Jacobs asked me to spearhead this effort, I knew that I could not do this without his help. One year ago, he put me in touch with most of you in this room."

Latrice's eyes wonder to the back and she sees Rick. Their eyes connect in their most special way. But the Senator catches it as well.

Latrice begins to speak to her group of people assembled, "The time is right. And more importantly, the motive is right. As I look around, yeah it even feels right. World hunger has many faces. Many of them you know. I won't bother naming. But this gathering is about channeling the resources of our government towards more fruitful humanitarian efforts."

She's grabbing the attention of her audience more and more with every spoken word. Rick, in his simple jeans, boots, t shirt and blazer from the day, has found himself an easy seat on the very back row.

Latrice carries on, "The total cost to launching men into space since 1969 is around 200 billion dollars.

That averages out to be 1.5 billion over the course of the entire program. These missions were supposed to build hope that we could pioneer life in outer space... out there, I guess."

She gets quite a few chuckles that sit under sophistication.

Latrice continues, "Think about it. Hope is a powerful emotion that works best when it is attached to something meaningful."

And from the back of the room and with his arms folded, Rick interjects, "Meaningful or just simply tangible?"

The audience quickly turns around to see who made that unexpected comment. They do not know how to judge it quite yet. Rick's voice is so extremely manly, charismatic, and easy on any ear.

She thinks to herself, "Rick, why can't you just sit your ass still and keep quiet?"

She replies, "Both."

Rick elaborates, "Excuse me for interjecting. But why would you want to exchange one program for another?

Senator Jacobs turns around and responds, "We will take a few questions in a moment."

Rick responds, "I thought this was an interactive forum, like all the Senator's skits."

The audience chuckles.

Latrice is mad because she knows exactly what he's doing, "Rickland, it would be great if you could just hold on to your question for right now."

Rick responds, "This is a waste of taxpayers' money."

Senator Jacobs gives an eye signal to his Secret Service. One gets the signal and then he signals the other two. And before he knows it, Rick is being approached by three Secret Service detail.

Latrice sees them coming toward Rick. "No hold it. He's right. This should be interactive."

Rick's radical approach to expressing himself has the entire room on edge now.

Rick says, "Relax. It's just a forum."

The several rows of people turn back and forth between Latrice and Rick. Ron Jacobs is so pissed he doesn't know what to do.

Rick looks directly at Latrice and just looks at her. And it's as if they were the only two people in the room. She hears his thoughts. "If you take the hope out of any cause, what you are left with is something that might not be worth fighting for."

She hates it when he speaks like this. But she knows that he wasn't speaking. He was thinking. But he may as well have been speaking. Either way, its irritating to her. "This was supposed to be my moment to speak about what was important to me."

And in this weird mysterious moment, that time isn't quite frozen completely, it's apparent that Rick's mission was accomplished. The space program that he seems to be passionately connected to needed to be spoken up for. And it might have come at the expense of his woman's happiness in doing so.

Latrice is furious.

Rick gets up and leaves. He knows that he pissed Latrice off who still stands at the podium, lost for words. And the Washington Times and the Huffington Post photographers seize this moment by snapping a photo of her with a tense facial expression.

And those camera flashes take Latrice back into the cloud.

Ch 52

Kaylandria asks. "So you were at odds with Rick."

Latrice responds, "He's crazy. I did nothing to him!"

Latrice is levitating and finds herself floating backwards to the inner wall of the cloud. She places her arms out horizontally and then slips them into pockets in the wall as if it were a coat, or sleeves to a straightjacket.

No one told her to do that. But her emotions were allowed to live and keep her honest. This cloud offers one the safety of a haven. A powerful feeling of abandonment comes to visit her once more from that moment.

The cloud itself now bears the responsibility of taking Latrice deeper into the complex air structure. She then hears the next sound. Latrice reluctantly continues with her last thought.

Kaylandria's voice says, "Deeper."

Ch 53

The strange cloud takes Latrice into yet another moment in her relationship past.

The organizer of the event is Senator Ron Jacobs of Florida. The Senator gets too close up on Latrice. And he's had a little too much to drink.

Latrice was a resourceful woman who was reaching very hard to succeed, but almost a little too hard. Rick knew this and would often ask himself and her, "Where is your line?"

"How could you ask that?"

Ricks responds, "I have to ask."

"Well you shouldn't have to."

"Why would I not? That is my responsibility to you."

"And I love you for that. Even when I don't ask, you're always looking out for me."

Rick would realize her truth of where his relationship was heading when Senator Ron Jacobs introduced Latrice to someone who was loaded with money who was looking to create a non-profit interest group based in DC. His name was Odyssey.

Rick had to be really savvy with this guy. At the same time that he was connecting Latrice with Odyssey, Senator Jacobs had offered Rick a career move of a lifetime down in Florida at NASA.

Rick had no choice to be excited. All of his questions and doubts about who he was as a man with concrete purpose were finally being settled. He could finally breathe.

"See. I told you." goes Latrice.

Rick stands there with his hands in his pocket, silent. And he goes silent for the rest of the night. Latrice notices his spirit going dark.

"You okay?"

Rick responds, "Huh? Oh yeah."

But the same night of this shoe-in , unadvertised career move, Rick has a dream. He pops up from his sleep. And he cannot go back to sleep. Latrice rakes her wonderful nails while rubbing her warm hands on the lower portion of his back as he sits on the side of the bed.

"What's wrong?"

"Nothing."

"What's wrong?"

"I had a dream."

"You're sweating."

Rick says nothing.

"Talk to me honey."

And he does. In this dream, Rick was shown that he would blow up in a shuttle explosion just beyond the ionosphere. He would do press coverage, flight simulations, rigorous training, the whole nine beforehand. But the result would still be his death.

Latrice says while her cheek rests on the cool side of the pillow, "You're probably just excited baby. Come on. Come back to sleep. Come on. Will you let me hold you?"

The question was more like a statement. Latrice has a very specific way of holding Rick that imposes the most gentle, the most nurturing, soft womanly touch that he certainly loves responding to.

Cradled by Latrice's warmth and the softness of their feather down comforter and creamy jersey sheets, Rick gets aroused by the tenderness of her method of resolve. His confession gives way to a transparency that allows his guard to come down. And those emotions turn to feelings. Those feelings create a nice and wonderful hard erection. And Latrice, who notices everything, is turned on. She does an excellent job in arousing her man when he is honest, silent, strong, and tender. Their inner beings may now have their way with one another.

The other part of the dream that Rick did not share was that he had seen a bridge of light after the shuttle had exploded. And on that bridge were his wife and children. The reason Rick chose not to share it was because he could not see or make out any of these people's faces.

Rick made love to Latrice as if he were searching for the meaning of life itself. He saw her as a passageway, a question.

On her back with every thrust, her beautiful eyes would look up at him and she would think, "Who are you?"

For the first time in that very moment, it was a struggle, but Latrice was allowing herself to understand the essence of their connection.

But in Rick's mind, he was wrestling with what was placed in his spirit. "A bridge... a bridge of blue light." Indeed, the bridge was made of blue light. And it was beautiful indeed.

A little while later, they were in the bed and their entanglement was beginning to loosen as they find their normal spots in the bed. And Rick was caught between who was touching him in the natural and what had been revealed to him in his spirit.

They would both think, "'I'll just have to see how everything will play out."

At NASA Rick would become the assistant deputy director of the organization. So before Rick would go too deep into any guilty feelings, Latrice helped him to take full advantage of transitioning.

Rick says, "What do you mean you're not coming?"

Latrice responds, "Odyssey needs me here in the new office."

"I get it."

"Do you?"

The plan that Latrice wanted was for Rick to hold his new position back in the DC area within a year.

At that point, the new powerful non-profit would have all of its legs to stand on. But the weekend visits began getting spaced apart one month into the new plan. And Rick began figuring it all out. And this was not what Latrice had asked for either.

Her husband was slipping out of the picture. And it was really beginning to hurt. But Latrice wasn't answering or taking phone calls either. Her cell number changed.

And then one day Rick reached out and said, "I'm being asked to take the last shuttle up to space. When I come down, I'll start the new Assistant Deputy Director job."

Rick was starting to accept the new reality of he and Latrice being so far apart, "Well, let's just see how things shape up. We should probably take a minute to figure out all of the goals that need attention."

Latrice realized that she hates it all, "I can't stand when you speak that corporate, space, political talk with me." And he knows it. But Rick evolved into a smooth talker when he realized that all he had was his vision. And this was Senator Ron Jacob's plan all along, to separate Latrice from Rick.

"So that's it. You feel like I left you and so now you're making me pay?" She sighs, and just sits silent.

Now it's Latrice that feels so helpless and abandoned. "You put that stupid job over me."

And it is now driving Latrice insane. "Listen, Odyssey wants you to head up areas that you've been dying to get your hand on. And guess what? They're in DC."

Rick doesn't really give her the answer that she was looking for. He's probably figured out that Latrice has gone to Odyssey and/or the Senator and pulled the necessary strings to get him back. Whether it happens or not, Rick has now found solace at Cape Canaveral, FL.

"Listen, I can navigate my own career."

And that saddens Latrice. "Okay."

The voice of the Creator tells Kaylandria, "Enough."

Ch 54

Latrice is released from the grasps of the wall of the cloud.

Kaylandria appears just in time to catch Latrice as she falls to the floor. "You did well."

The enchanted mystical walls of the clouds have gathered the necessary information from Latrice.

Kaylandria looks down at Latrice as her head rests on Kaylandria's lap, "The strange house in which you have traveled into not only knows you better, but now knows the world in which you must now live."

Kaylandria helps her out of the cloud and now ushers Latrice in a certain direction.

"Come with me. But say nothing. For you now have the power to hear in places where you are not present."

Cн 55

Latrice then begins hearing the voices of Asani, Five, and Bowers. None are within sight. And Kaylandria continues taking her in this strange new direction. Latrice has been rendered helpless to her senses, accept hearing, to the point where all that she can do is absorb and process.

Meanwhile, Five and Asani are walking back to Bowers' house.

Five is heavy in thought. "Let me share something about your father."

And Asani's eyes brighten up.

"You're father's name was Antonias, King Antonias. He was the ruler of his people, our people, for somewhat of a short period of time. But in his time as king, Antonias brought in more new beginnings for his people than any other ruler. A remnant even called your father "The Genesis King".

Latrice's ear is actively engaged in this conversation as Kaylandria carries her across the Sky of Erydia.

Then with her eyes still closed, Latrice sees Five trying to kill Asani, and hearing him say, "It is such a pity that it has to come to this."

Latrice's eyes open. "We have to stop."

And Kaylandria stops in midair. She knows what Latrice is seeing. "It is time to make a decision."

Latrice says, "What do you mean? I need to get back to where he is."

Kaylandria says, "Yes, you are seeing that Asani is in trouble."

"How do we stop Five? There has to be a way."

Kaylandria says, "The question is what must be done by you?"

Latrice shakes her head. "There you go speaking in riddles again."

"Our journey can stop here. And you can rush to his aid."

Latrice sighs in relief.

"Or you can trust that he will make the right decision to save himself."

"What?"

Kaylandria continues, "If you allow him to save himself, you get to continue on your own journey."

Latrice says, "But…"

"If you do not, you will have come all this way to not see what is in store for you."

Latrice is so far away, but she looks in Asani's direction.

Kaylandria does absolutely nothing. The weight of the decision must fall on Latrice.

Latrice sighs and extends her hand to Kaylandria. They resume their flight course.

Kaylandria says, "From this point moving forward, their conversation, you may still continue to hear them as it continues to please you."

Cн 56

Five takes the rods and disappears into the cave, leaving Asani on his back, yet again.

Five makes his way back onto the bridge of the dark flagship of Gonondrius. "My lord, here are the Rods of the Yeswe'."

He remains hidden in the shadow of his own command seat, seeing nothing but his incredibly sinister smile. Gonondrius says, "Good. Proceed with the next phase."

Five makes his way over to the space craft's helm. "Plot a course to the Milky Way galaxy, destination, Earth."

It is so frightening to actually see what sort of creature is at the helm. Even Five even has to shun his own little face. For Gonondrius had no desire to be reminded of what he once was when he was much younger.

Meanwhile, Asani makes it to the house. And Bowers greets him on the porch.

Bowers is in great expectation for a curse to be lifted. "That was the bargain. That was the agreement. I should have known better."

The questions, the stories, the lack of answers, it doesn't make sense. And in the midst of this conversation of confusion, Asani loses his composure. It gets Bowers' attention as he sits nursing his head. He throws any caution to the wind and gets in Bowers face, yoking him up by his shirt collar. "Okay, I want some answers and I want them right now!"

Bowers smirks. "Oh, you're serious?"

He can feel the familiar strength of his father clinching collar of shirt ever so tight.

"All right let go."

He pushes Bowers out of his hands.

"Right before you awakened, Five and Rhaija put a curse on me. They did it so that he could eventually get his hands on those rods that you so generously handed over to Five."

Asani interjects, "I know. I mean if Five wasn't supposed to have them, then why did you…".

Bowers sighs and over talks him, "Yeah, yeah, I know. Why…"

Asani interjects, "Why didn't you keep them away? So the first question I have is, Why…".

Bowers interjects, "Yeah, yeah, I know. See, Five can only appear to the true holder of the sacred Rods a total of 3 times."

Asani is floored, "Why didn't you tell me?"

And Bowers is really ashamed, but frustrated at the same time that this naive young man is questioning him. "It's the damn curse. I couldn't do anything. And if I told you, he would have found out. And how was I supposed to know that you didn't know anything about the Rods?"

But Bowers then remembers. He altered Asani's stasis chamber informational routine. "There are things that you know, and a lot of things that you do not know that you have to know. Unfortunately those things that you do not know are partly my fault. But again, I wasn't myself."

Asani looks at Bowers intently, "Who are you anyway? And how long was I asleep."

Bowers takes a second and gathers his thoughts. "Prior to you awakening, the Spirit Rhaija was convinced by Five to cast this spell, a curse of forgetfulness upon me. I had specific instructions to lead, guide, and direct you in all the ways of truth. And that truth is who you are. You are…"

All of sudden, Bower's experience's a pain in his upper spine, "Uhh!"

And he falls to his knees, trying to reach around but he cannot. Asani tries to help him up, but finds it difficult because Bowers is gasping for air. The sharpness of the pain was anticipated by Bowers. And all of a sudden he coughs. And Bowers coughs once more. And then on a third time, he was able to release a green misty toxin from his body. Asani looks perplexed as the gas rises into the air and then dissipates.

Bowers, while still on one knee, looks up at Asani and says, "Help me up."

Asani does as requested. And Bowers just looks at him. "Did you have to give him all of the damn rods?"

"You gave them to me to give to him."

Bowers sighs.

And just like that, Bowers goes back to doing his typical day to day routine. He heads back down stairs in his strange one story ranch style house to where all of the servers are.

Asani follows. "Well, aren't you going to go after him?"

Bowers says nothing.

"So what just happened? What does Five have?"

Bowers explains, "The holder of all five rods has the power to move an entire star from one position to another."

And Asani thinks, "Why in the world would he want to do that?"

"He's doing it because he is a little man. And he's doing the bidding of an even bigger little man. Five could only appear to you a total of three (3) times in the manner in which he did, through portholes. Those portholes were provided by the Spirit Rhaija who he negotiated with in order to spare his own worthless life."

Asani erupts, "Why didn't you just stop him?"

"Because I was abducted, drugged, and seduced. Stop asking me silly questions."

"When?"

"Asani, probably a day or so before you were awakened."

"So, I don't understand. Where are we now?"

"I'm afraid I can't tell you."

"Why not?"

"I'm afraid I can't tell you that."

"Why not?

"Just know that we're safe."

What Bowers wants to explain to Asani has everything to do with Antonias' last set of instructions before he died.

Bowers says to Asani, "Let's say that prior to you awaking, some or all of the rods were used."

Asani replies, "Look, no more riddles."

But all Bowers can think about is the promise that he made to Antonias in his final moments of life on Ghanima.

Asani says, "This will remain a secret."

Bowers replies, "Oh I know it will, because the future of our kingdom rests on it."

Asani gets agitated. "What kingdom?"

Bowers continues on. "Okay now, when you have four rods…"

"You're just going to talk right over me."

"Who needs the explanation, you or me? The holder of 4 rods can move one land mass from one place to another."

CH 57

At the same time, Latrice is asking, "How is this possible? Who exactly is Asani? And what Kingdom does he come from?"

And just as Bowers did with Asani, Kaylandria ignores the direct line of questioning administered by Latrice. However she does say, "Are you familiar with the term PANGEA?"

Latrice says, "Of course, that's the uh... land mass... yeah where all the continents were together, until they drifted apart."

Kaylandria says, "Correct, but the continents drifted apart on Earth because the Guardians left their posts. Five, who you were hearing talking to Asani, wants to bring the continents back together once more.

Latrice sighs, "This just keeps getting more and more confusing. What Guardians?"

Kaylandria responds, "The original Kingdom from four and half billion years ago will be united once more. And the people will be easier to rule from one centralized location. It is Five's assignment to see this plan come to pass. Your friend Asani's mission is to stop Five from ever executing that plan, but he is very unclear of it because of the spell placed upon his guardian, Bowers, who was to give him those instructions."

Latrice asks, "Well, why can't we help him."

"Because it is not our assignment to help him."

Latrice says, "Well, if you were to ask me, these assignments are sounding like a waste of time."

"Try to understand. They must figure this out for themselves."

Latrice responds, "I'm hearing things that make me ask questions. Does Asani desire to rule as his father once did? Who is pressuring him either way?"

Kaylandria replies, "Good. But the main question that you must answer first is what role will you play in this?"

Latrice never considered that.

As Kaylandria takes Latrice through low altitudes of flying over a beautiful desert, Latrice goes back to concentrating and listening.

"Good Latrice. There is so much to learn."

Ch 58

Lost within this endless space and time of this strange House of Erydia, Latrice goes back to listening. And within a quick moment, she finds the voice of Bowers, speaking to Asani.

"For example, I relocated the land that this house sits on prior to you waking up. Then I went back to resting when I was done".

Asani asks, "What? Why?"

"I can't tell you."

Bowers does however say some of the same things that Kaylandria just told Latrice. "Our original Kingdom used to be one large land mass. But it was so vast that it was impossible for your grandfather, King Gakuru, to manage it. So after experiencing its size first hand, he divided his Kingdom into 14 territories and assigned 14 rulers to uphold Gakuru's law while protecting its people. It was simply beautiful at first. Each ruler would manage the affairs of their land. And each ruler would take his cares back to the ears of the King. But when the King had decided to gather his people and depart from the Earth, trusting the enticing words of a foreign woman, he did so with the plan in mind to leave all 14 rulers in place."

Meanwhile, Kaylandria interrupts Latrice's meditating thoughts. "Now, when this actually happened, it caught my attention, just as it is catching yours. You see, on this Earth's continuum, over four billion years ago, I was the King's Spiritual Advisor. A prophesy came through my voice that day."

The same Kaylandria who is with Latrice once said to King Gakuru, "The rulers will all leave their assigned posts. But one of the territories will bring the 14 back together once more."

And then all of a sudden, a different voice enters Latrice's mind, one that speaks with a different cadence, however vaguely familiar. The voice is rich, ever so strong, and authoritative.

Cʜ 59

Kaylandria says, "Latrice, I think that I should tell you something."

"Tell me what?"

"This is the moment where you must make a decision. Either you become the caretaker of this world. Or you can actually become the Queen of the Earth."

Latrice couldn't believe her ears. And she smiles in amazement. "Queen... of the Earth? Well, eat your heart out Michelle Obama. When did we ever have a Queen? Stop playing with me."

"I assure you that I am not."

Latrice responds, "Well wait. If I become the caregiver..."

"Caretaker."

"Right, caretaker… that sounds like some retirement home position."

"Well you are in a home. Remember?"

Latrice says, "Right. Well, how long do I have to make up my mind?"

Kaylandria looks up at the sun. "You time is winding up now."

"Queen. Hmm… can I see who the King is first? I mean the offer sounds nice, but…"

"Believe me, you will not be disappointed."

"Yeah, but can I see him?"

Kaylandria replies, "You are making this too complicated. Allow me to assist you. If you choose to be the caretaker of this House…"

"A caretaker… right?"

"Then you will not be permitted to experience the ability to connect in a romantic sense."

Latrice takes a second to think about that. "You mean you ain't getting' none?"

Kaylandria's confused look is enough to answer that question.

Latrice says, "Well wouldn't that just suck? What kind of life would that be?"

"But if you choose the other and live out this life being Queen, well… let's just say your options become limitless."

"Now that's what I'm talkin' about!"

But just before Latrice gives her a high five, she stops to think. "But what about Asani? I mean I would like to see him again."

Kaylandria says, "You must trust your heart. And take the path that it truly desires to take. If he is where your true desire resides, then consider what you have experienced and what I have shared in this House of Erydia."

Latrice goes silent.

"Close your eyes. Now choose."

Latrice says, "Wait. Now hold up. Now what exactly are my choices?"

Kaylandria sighs. "If you become the overseer of the House, then all of its enchanting mystery are yours and yours alone to guard over."

"Sounds like a job. I'm sure that I would be reporting to someone, right?"

Kaylandria says, "Correct."

"Well, who would that be? These are all legitimate questions."

"Oh they are, but you will receive your answers based on…"

Latrice cuts over her, "The option I choose, right?"

"I am awaiting your answer."

Latrice is faced with a choice that no one else has ever had. She knows that she has to get this decision right.

Kaylandria awaits Latrice's response.

Latrice says, "Will I be able to touch or have even have normal interactions?"

"You mean with someone like Asani?"

"No. For the danger is too great. So much would be at risk for a mere few stolen moments."

Latrice responds, "Okay, all right. I got it. I mean don't you have a desire to be wanted?"

Kaylandria looks at Latrice with a certain intensity that she has restrained.

Latrice says, "Okay, well that's out. A girl has to be touched. So explain in detail this second option."

"You would be Queen."

Latrice responds, "I don't remember studying in history class any Queens of the entire Earth."

"That is because I made sure that none were recorded."

"Queen of the Earth, when?"

Kaylandria responds, "Just about the time of the Earth's inception."

"Which would be how long ago?"

"Oh, I would say approximately four and a half billion years ago."

Latrice looks at Kaylandria as if she's crazy. And she smiles. "Come on. Really? Like with T-Rex's and all that scary stuff?"

Kaylandria says, "Trust me."

"What about technology?"

"Trust me."

"And electricity?"

"Trust me."

"Is there a King?"

"Yes."

"Will I love him?"

"Choose."

Latrice takes several deep breaths and looks onto the lay of the land. She has made her choice but she's said nothing. Her pretty eyelids fall shut and Latrice holds herself. She has taken into account all of what has happened in her life, all the way up til now.

Kaylandria comes up from behind Latrice and is hesitant, but she gently palms the back of Latrice's head. "This may not be wise, but you will be permitted to keep your memories."

"Well who wouldn't want me to?"

"The Creator."

"The creator of what?"

"Of us of course."

Latrice says, "So the creator of the universe is okay with me becoming Queen but he doesn't want me to have my memory."

"I never asked, but I'm pretty sure that that is how He feels."

"This is too much. Y'all can have this."

Kaylandria says nothing.

"Why am I doing this anyway?" Latrice asks.

"The better question is what keeps you moving forward?"

Latrice says, "Because I hate my life."

Kaylandria responds, "Then trust yourself to take this step, and then another, until you have no more steps to take. Only then will you find the life that you believe you lost."

Latrice turns around and hugs Kaylandria, "You will keep your memory so that you can make sense of what you are about to experience. Along with that, you will have full awareness of your new life in real time as it is happening. Your brain as a result will utilize its full ability to process your past, which will be everyone's future, while living in your new present, which is the Earth's past. Got it?"

Latrice says, "That just made my head hurt. I think."

"Good. Remember you cannot share anything from your former life in this time. This is going to be a rather trying mental exercise. You have impressed me. I did not think that you would be so open."

Latrice says nothing.

"You seem rather distant. Are you okay?"

Latrice responds, "I'm assuming that you'll be somewhere around if I do not understand something."

"If this moves too fast or if you find yourself confused about something, you have only to speak the words, 'Knowledge of Erydia... grant me your wisdom'. But do not overuse this gift. If the powers of Erydia feel that you can figure something out on your own, you will hear nothing from me. More than likely, when you utter those words, our normal rapport will resume. I will acknowledge you as Latrice. Otherwise, you will be acknowledged as Queen Sureia."

Latrice responds, "Queen Who?"

"Are you ready?"

Latrice takes a deep breath to consider all of this. "So if I'm Queen Sureia and when I utter the words Knowledge of Erydia... grant me your wisdom, you will appear if Erydia feels it warrants a discussion."

"Right."

"Otherwise, I am on my own."

"You will do fine. Close your eyes."

Latrice closes her eyes as she once again raises her eyebrow of skepticism. "I'm a grown woman. I don't think my name is going to be changing at this point in my life, queen or no queen."

Ch 60

Her eyes open. And Latrice finds herself standing in the midst of a beautiful tropical paradise. She looks down at herself and her attire has changed altogether. She is draped with lavender fabric, smoother than the finest silk, accented with tasteful quality gold dust, and no shoes, because the grass supports her every step without getting her feet nasty nor wet.

She looks around and instantly becomes afraid, "Kaylandria? Where are you? Knowledge of Erydia.. grant me your wisdom."

Nothing happens. Latrice turns around and tries to find her bearings. She so is much on guard. It's as if the tall trees have a thousand eyes all on her. It is unbearably quiet, not one sound. She's never heard herself breathe so clearly.

"Your highness, are you all right?" asks a strange strapping man in a gold suit of armor, and completely ready for combat.

Latrice asks, "Me?"

"You had walked off away from my sight." He says.

"I'm sorry, do I know you?"

The kind soldier kneels down and offers Latrice a tiny container. "Did you step onto any brahciny (worse than poison ivy) by accident? If so, I have the antidote right here."

"No. I am fine."

"Good, then it is time for us to depart."

"To where?"

"To the King, of course, Queen Sureia. He is expecting you."

The soldier escorts Latrice on a walk just through the thick of the brush where Kaylandria and a man are standing in quiet discussion.

As Latrice gets closer she hears the voice of King Gakuru, and he says to Kaylandria "You speak in riddles. What do you mean back together again? Not that I should have to explain myself to you or anyone else. I gave you time to speak because every voice deserves to be heard at least once. But I place careful time into my choices, especially in the case of Kingdom matters."

Latrice has made her way through the brush and Gakuru turns around. And Latrice's eyes pop wide open. "Rick?"

Gakuru gives her a perplexed look, "And what exactly is a Rick, my dear Sureia?"

Latrice stands in utter disbelief as she has been transported to a time period that shortly follows the inception of the Earth.

Bowers and Asani are nowhere to be found, now that Latrice has left the House of Erydia. The mystery of their exact whereabouts must be revealed to Latrice before Five can figure out how to use the Rods of the Yeswe'.